W9-CIJ-699

MURDER DELAYED

A Selection of Recent Titles by Roderic Jeffries

AN AIR OF MURDER *
ARCADIAN DEATH
AN ARTISTIC WAY TO GO
DEFINITELY DECEASED *
AN ENIGMATIC DISAPPEARANCE
AN INTRIGUING MURDER *
MURDER DELAYED *
MURDER'S LONG MEMORY
RELATIVELY DANGEROUS
SEEING IS DECEIVING *
A SUNNY DIAPPEARANCE *
TOO CLEVER BY HALF

* *available from Severn House*

MURDER DELAYED

Roderic Jeffries

This first world edition published in Great Britain 2006 by
SEVERN HOUSE PUBLISHERS LTD of
9–15 High Street, Sutton, Surrey SM1 1DF.
This first world edition published in the USA 2006 by
SEVERN HOUSE PUBLISHERS INC of
595 Madison Avenue, New York, N.Y. 10022.

British Library Cataloguing in Publication Data

Jeffries, Roderic, 1926-
Murder delayed. - (An Inspector Alvarez novel)
1. Alvarez, Enrique, Inspector (Fictitious character) - Fiction
2. Police - Spain - Majorca - Fiction
3. Majorca (Spain) - Fiction
4. Detective and mystery stories
I. Title
823.9'14 [F]

ISBN 0-7278-6336-3

Typeset by Palimpsest Book Production Ltd.,
Polmont, Stirlingshire, Scotland.
Printed and bound in Great Britain by
MPG Books Ltd., Bodmin, Cornwall.

One

Detective Sergeant Raft entered the CID general room in a rush.

'Morning, Sarge,' Clumber said.

'It's a bloody awful morning: cold and raining like the second flood.'

If Raft ended up in heaven, he would quickly find cause for complaint, Clumber thought.

'Where's Stan?'

'Following up the mugging in Bracket Street.'

'Bert?'

'Reported in sick; thinks he's caught mumps from his kid.'

'More likely, sleeping sickness. The Guv'nor's had a call from Finch and Abbott, a financial-advisory set-up, concerning an employee, Michael Faber. Seems he's nicked four hundred and ninety-nine thousand pounds and disappeared. Why the hell didn't he take one more and make it a half-million?'

'No sense of symmetry.'

'Speak to the boss-man and get all the details.'

'Where's the firm hang out?'

'High Street, just past Marks and Sparks.'

'It's here, in town?'

'No. Stornoway.'

'It's just I didn't reckon there were enough people in Tistford with sufficient loose change to need a financial adviser to tell them what to do with it.'

'You think there are still some honest men around? Get moving. Check with the firm, see if there's anything in his home that's interesting, talk to neighbours, the usual.'

'Where does he live?'

'How would I know? If you're really bright, you'll ask someone who does.' Raft turned and left.

Clumber looked at the files and forms on his desk. An army marched on its stomach, the police on paperwork. It would have to be cleared before he left for home that evening, so he'd be late and Betty would moan.

He took the lift down to the ground floor and went out into the heavy rain; by the time he reached the CID car, he echoed the sergeant's judgement: it was a bloody awful morning. The Ford was old, reluctant to start, and the heater no longer worked.

There was no parking allowed in High Street even though the road was wide. He would have left the car outside Marks and Spencer had the relationship between uniform and CID not deteriorated to the extent that the first PC to see the parked car and identify it as CID would report it to a traffic warden.

The nearest car park was two roads away and a notice said it was full. In no mood to accept that, he drove in and almost immediately a car backed out of a bay and left. His pleasure at having successfully defied the sign quickly evaporated as he walked through the rain to the offices of Finch and Abbott.

The woman behind the reception desk was young, heavily made up and she had styled, frizzy hair. He thought her a smart dish; Betty would have called her tarty. He introduced himself. She spoke on an internal phone, replaced the receiver, stood. 'Would you like to come with me?'

He said he'd be delighted. Her expression became scornful. He followed her into a large office, furnished with quiet luxury – a room to inspire respect and trust. No doubt Langham's manner would normally have amplified such character, but right then it suggested panic.

'Thank God you're here! I never for one second thought it possible. He always seemed so solid. I can remember the day he saved us from a bad mistake . . .'

'Perhaps we can take things one at a time, Mr Langham.'

'I'm sorry. I am very disturbed. Please sit down.'

Clumber settled on a luxuriously upholstered chair, which received rather than supported him. 'If you'll tell me all that's happened.'

It was a story well known to all police forces: the hard-working employee who had been with the firm long enough to be regarded as competent and completely trustworthy. Faber had handled the firm's computer work.

Langham said miserably, 'No one was keeping much of a check on him because . . . well, there didn't seem to be any reason to and he was so expert it was difficult to keep up with what he was doing.'

He had produced facts, figures and graphs, enabling the partners to give first-class advice to the clients and they had found his work invaluable . . . until he had failed to arrive at the office, phone calls to his home were unanswered, and one of their most important clients had queried the valuation of his portfolio. A frantic internal investigation, aided by a computer expert, had shown four hundred and ninety-nine thousand pounds had disappeared from clients' accounts. After thirty-two years in which the firm had gained a reputation any investment outfit in the City would have respected, it was now ruined . . .

'He's not answering his phone at home?'

'We've tried again and again.'

'Have you any idea where he might be now?'

'D'you think there'd be so much terrible worry if we did?'

'Of course not, Mr Langham. What I'm wondering is if you, or anyone else in the firm, might have inadvertently learned something which could suggest where he might have gone into hiding.'

'He never spoke about himself. He was someone who . . . Difficult to explain, but he seemed to build a wall around himself.'

'Because he'd been planning the robbery for a long time?'

'I suppose that's possible. Only . . .'

'Yes?'

'He never gave that impression.'

'He wouldn't,' Clumber said, managing not to voice his sarcasm. 'If he was intelligent – which he must be in his job – he'll have accepted that the moment the loss of money was discovered, he would be suspect numero uno so he had to hide his tracks from the beginning. What I'd like to do now is question your staff before I check out his home.'

'I'm quite certain they're all trustworthy.'

'Which is what you thought Faber.'

'True,' Langham said sadly.

After leaving the offices, Clumber went into Marks and Spencer and bought Betty's favourite dish: chicken Kiev. It was to be hoped that his thoughtfulness would mute her annoyance at his working hours.

Two Oaks was in the village of Eddington. It was a ragstone building that had originally been four cottages which lacked all amenities other than cold taps; with the aid of a grant, four had been turned into two and the two modernized.

As Clumber turned away from the front door, there was a call from across a privet hedge.

'He ain't there.'

He turned to face an elderly man with a face leathered

by years of working in the open. 'So when was the last time you saw him?'

'What's that to you?'

'Detective Constable Clumber, county CID.'

'Well, I never!'

'Can I have a word with you?'

'Ain't that what you're doing?'

'It would be more comfortable in the dry.'

'You youngsters can't take a drop of rain.'

It wasn't now raining buckets, but certainly more than drops.

'Come on in, then, and the missus can brew up a cuppa.'

He walked up the short path to the road and along to the other gate. The small front garden was colourful, despite the sodden conditions – a sharp contrast to the weed-infested one outside Faber's house. In the kitchen, warmed by a Reburn stove, a plump, cheerful woman, dressed haphazardly, said a cup of tea wouldn't be long and did he like chocolate biscuits?

He left forty-five minutes later, having drunk two cups of tea, eaten four chocolate digestives, and learned little other than that Faber kept himself to himself, at weekends frequently drove up to see his elderly aunt and give her what help he could, and when he did entertain, it was always men. He spent the next hour and a half talking to the occupants of the four houses nearby, the last of which was a timber-framed farmhouse, the kind of home Betty would insist they buy when they won the lottery. They told him nothing new.

Back at divisional HQ, he reported to Raft.

'He's gay?'

'That's the general verdict. And in most cases, since the neighbours are all pretty ancient, a disapproving one.'

'Any chance of identifying a partner?'

'Not a hope. None of them was recognized.'

'So our only lead is ancient aunty?'

'That's it.'

'Where in Birmingham does she live?'

'No one knows.'

'What's her name?'

'June or Jane.'

'Surname?'

'He never mentioned it.'

'We're looking beaten before we start.'

'Jarvis, the old boy in the other semi, says that whenever Faber went on holiday, he came back as brown as a berry and he once said that when he retired, he'd move abroad and live where it was sunny more often than rainy.'

'So where did he chase the sun?'

'Jarvis couldn't say.'

'Faber must have given a hint.'

'If he did, Jarvis doesn't remember what it was.'

'And the neighbours couldn't add anything?'

'No.'

'You checked his house?'

'It's locked.'

'You're telling me you couldn't find a door or window that was poorly secured?'

'Reckoned I'd better consult with you first.'

Raft looked at his wristwatch. 'It's not worth going for a warrant and in any case I have to be with the Guv'nor in half an hour. And when that's over, drive out to Itchley . . . We'll have a look around his place tomorrow morning.'

'It's Saturday.'

'So?'

'It's my weekend off.'

'It was.'

He should have also bought two packs of lemon pie, Clumber thought gloomily, remembering Betty's plans for the weekend.

* * *

After a thorough search of the house, they were certain that it was bare of personal papers and of anything which could have offered clues as to where Faber might have fled. Raft used his doubtful skills to relock the outside back door.

'That was a sodding waste of time,' Clumber said bitterly.

'If you could learn that if a job's worth doing, it's worth doing properly, you might stand a chance of becoming an efficient detective.' Raft pocketed the tool he had been using, which looked like a dentist's drill.

They rounded the corner of the house. As they approached the wooden gate, in need of repainting, a post-office van drew up and a postman climbed out, letters in his hand.

'If those are for Faber, he's away and won't be coming back,' Clumber said.

'He's given us no change of address.'

'Hardly surprising.'

'You've a lot to say about him.'

'Local CID.'

'Like to show your card?'

Clumber brought out his warrant card from his inside coat pocket.

'Sorry, mate, but one has to be careful these days.'

'Now we're introduced, care to have a word?'

The postman, whose face was extraordinarily round, smiled. 'Are you giving me an option?'

'Let's get back in the lee of the house; the wind's straight off the Arctic.'

'Too right. Might be January, not March.'

They walked round to the back of the house and this not only gave them protection from the icy wind, it also, since the sun was shining intermittently, offered an illusion of spring.

'We're wondering where Faber is right now?' Clumber said.

'So what's up?'

'He's a witness and we need his evidence,' he answered vaguely. 'Maybe you can help us contact him?'

'I couldn't say where he is unless it's at his aunty's.'

'The one who he frequently visits?'

'As far as I know, she's his only one.'

'Do you know where she lives or her surname?'

'Sorry, mate.'

'He doesn't get any letters from her?'

'Don't remember one.'

'Did he ever talk about the places he goes to on holiday?'

'Usually never said more than "Good morning."'

'Did he ever get letters from abroad?'

'I can't remember any . . . Although come to think about it, there was one from a hotel.'

'Where?'

'Since there was an address on the back of the envelope, I can tell you: Llueso. Reminded me of the time Flo and me were there for a summer holiday. Little slice of heaven, she called it. We said we'd go back, but Tommy arrived and then Carol and that was the end of holidays abroad. No fun with babies.'

'Where's this place?'

'On the coast of Majorca.'

Raft was silent for a while, then said: 'You may have helped a lot.'

'The people's friend – that's our motto. So now do I just shove the letters through the box, same as usual, or take them back to the dead sack?'

'Nothing from Majorca amongst them, I suppose?'

The postman checked the three letters in his hand. 'Look like bills.'

Raft thanked him, said goodbye, led the way back to the Fiesta.

'Are you thinking maybe he's gone to this hotel in

Majorca?' Clumber asked, as he settled on the front passenger seat and secured the belt.

'It's not impossible. He'll know the place and that'll be a big plus when he's on the run and stressed.'

'But is he going to return to somewhere he's been known to visit? I mean, look at the way he cleared the house of everything so there's not a letter, a personalized phone list, a scrap of paper, to give anything away.'

Raft fired the engine, engaged first gear, and the car started with a jerk; he was a poor driver who rated himself a first-class one. 'If you think about it, the only person who could know he'd had contact with a hotel there was the postman and would he ever have reason to remember the letter and where it was from? What were the odds against us speaking to the postman who delivered the letter?'

'So what's the next move?'

'We put in a request to the police over there to find out if he's around.'

'He'll have travelled on a false passport.'

'We send a description.'

'There wasn't a photograph.'

'We check out if he's ever applied for a passport under his real name and get a photo from that.'

'He'll have been planning from the word go. He'll have travelled on false passports from the beginning so there'll be no trace of one issued to Faber in the records.'

'You think he's a bloody genius?'

'If you've successfully nicked half a million minus one, you're real smart. Sarge, if we ask the Spanish police to track him down when he'll be under a different name and the only description we can offer is what's given to us by people who'll disagree about everything, they won't be thanking us.'

'It'll be their problem, not ours.'

As they came up to a crossroads on the corner of which was a pub, a light drizzle began.

'I envy him,' Clumber said as Raft braked harshly, having misjudged the speed of a car coming in from the left, 'lying on the sand in the hot sun, an iced glassful of g and t in one hand, a luscious female in the other.'

'I thought you said he was gay?'

'I forgot.'

'That's your trouble. Always dreaming.' The oncoming car passed and Raft drove jerkily forward.

Two

As Enrique Alvarez stared through the window of the office, his eyelids grew heavy. The day was hot – hotter than usual for the last week in April – and this sapped a man's concentration.

The telephone awoke him. He stared at it with dislike. It continued to ring and, very reluctantly, he reached forward and lifted the receiver.

'Inspector Alvarez?'

He might have denied it had he not recognized the voice of Salas's secretary, an unfeeling woman who would have discerned and scorned his childish subterfuge. 'Speaking.'

'The superior chief will speak to you.' She could have been announcing the Prime Minister.

'Alvarez,' Salas said, as always speaking very quickly so that there was little break between words, 'I have received a request to locate an Englishman, name Michael Faber, wanted for questioning in respect of the fraud of five hundred thousand pounds. He is thought to be travelling under a false name and passport in this area. His description, lacking a photograph and therefore grossly inadequate, will be faxed to you in the next half-hour. You will find him.'

'Where is he staying?'

'That is not known.'

'But he is definitely in this area?'

'It is perfectly clear from the slipshod nature of the request that nothing is certain.'

'Then I don't see—'

'I am uninterested in your lack of vision.'

'But if I search for him without knowing his name and having a very poor description, I'll probably be wasting my time.'

'Something with which you will be familiar.'

'What I mean is—'

'On receipt of the fax, you will immediately make the identification, thereby showing the Cuerpo to be a highly efficient force, as compared to the English who have let this man slip through their fingers.'

'I do think—'

'Perhaps one day you will provide me with reassurance as to that.' He cut the connexion.

Alvarez replaced the receiver, slumped back in the chair. Trust Salas to issue an order without the slightest heed to the stress and work it must entail.

He looked at his watch: an hour before he was officially entitled to return home to his lunch; half an hour before it was reasonably safe to do so because then who, apart from Salas who had just rung, would disturb someone so close to a meal? . . . What would his cousin Dolores be cooking? When in a good mood, she produced miracles of culinary perfection. He could still remember the taste of the *menestra de habas de tudela* they had eaten the day before – beans with garlic, mint, saffron, almonds, artichoke hearts, boiled eggs, white wine and seasoning. But in a bad mood, she might well dish up food that would disgrace even a tourist restaurant. Was she likely to be in a good or a bad mood? She had been singing the previous evening, but this morning had been sharply critical of everyone. What had happened to change her mood so quickly? Would even she know the answer? As Josep Brey had written, 'Man can understand the awesome turmoil of a volcano better than that of a woman's mind.'

He closed his eyes. Today was Wednesday. Two and a half days to go before the weekend and he could relax . . .

He was woken when the door was opened with sufficient force to bang against the wall.

'Asleep on duty,' said the *cabo*. 'If you were in the army, you'd be shot.'

'I was not asleep, I was thinking; and I am not in the army.'

'Thank God for that or we would have to have the white flags ready. This has come through from Palma.' He put a single sheet of paper on the desk. 'Sweet dreams,' he said, as he left.

Alvarez picked up the paper and read:

> Michael Thomas Faber. Male. British Caucasian. Computer expert with special reference to financial matters. Age, around forty. Weight, between eleven and twelve stone; height between 5 foot 9 and 5 foot 11.

(How typical of the English to use their own absurd measures and not have the grace to translate them.)

> Forehead, high; hair, light brown, no sign of baldness; facial hair, none; chin, squarish; neck, medium length; lips, medium to thin and mouth unremarkable; eyes, dark brown, eyebrows, medium, slightly arched; nose, thin, straight; ears, close to head and rounded; distinctive marks, none; physical peculiarities, none. NB. The description of Faber is based on eyewitness accounts and as these differed in some respects, we have presented what we consider to be features most likely to be accurate. However, care should be taken in accepting any single feature as beyond doubt.

He put the fax down on the desk. It was acknowledged that the description was quite possibly – for which read probably – incorrect. So why bother to send it? Obviously because the English police were trying to exhibit efficiency while covering up inefficiency. History taught that the English were never to be trusted. One had only to remember the devious manner in which they had fought their naval battles – ignoring the customary tactics – to know that. And why no photographs?

He dialled Palma.

'Yes?' said Salas's secretary in her most commanding tones.

'Inspector Alvarez. I'd like to speak to the superior chief.'

'Wait.'

He waited.

'What is it?'

'Señor, I have just read—'

'Who's speaking?'

'Inspector Alvarez . . .'

'As if there could be any doubt!'

'Then . . . then why do you ask who I am?'

'Because the manner in which one makes an efficient report seems always to have been a complete mystery to you.'

'Señor, some time ago when I told you who I was you criticized me for wasting your time because your secretary had told you who was phoning. I presumed she would have done so today.'

'You are content to assume that what happened yesterday must inevitably happen today?'

'Then you do want me to identify myself and say who I am?'

'There are times when I wonder if you know.'

'Know what, señor?'

'Who you are.'

'I am beginning to wonder what I am supposed to do.'

'Was one of your relatives the director-general of the Cuerpo when you applied to join?'

'No, señor.'

'Then it is impossible to understand why you were accepted.'

There was a silence.

'Do you intend to tell my why you have phoned or am I supposed to guess?'

'The English have not included a photograph of Michael Faber in their fax.'

'As I mentioned.'

'Do you think they have forgotten?'

'Judge them not on your own level of competency.'

'But they might have done. Wouldn't it be an idea to ask them if—'

'It would not.'

'But without a photo of the Englishman, how am I going to identify him? They admit his description is based on eye-witness evidence and this was sometimes contradictory so an average has been given. Averages can be very wrong.'

'I have to explain to you how to conduct your case?'

'The season's started so there must be thousands of foreigners in the area and—'

'You lack the mental ability to determine a course of action? I will try to speak sufficiently simply for you to understand. You study each Englishman who arrived here on or after the nineteenth of the month – which, no doubt, you have forgotten was when Faber failed to report for work – and if he bears any resemblance to the description you have been given, you question him to determine his true identity.'

'That's an impossible task.'

'I am sorry to hear a member of the Cuerpo make so absurd a statement.'

'But it means talking to the staff in every hotel, aparthotel, hostel and letting agency in the area.'

'Of course.'

'That would involve a tremendous amount of work.'

'The thought frightens you?'

'I'll need help.'

'You are incapable of doing anything on your own?'

'Señor, on my own it will take so long to question so many people that inevitably word will get around about what I am doing. That must raise the possibility Faber realizes the police know he is in the area and he immediately leaves the island. In those circumstances, the English might scornfully judge we had been very clumsy in the way we had operated . . .'

'Detail three *policia* to help you in the initial stage of the investigation.' Salas rang off.

Three

'You're very quiet,' Dolores said as she held the ladle above the earthenware pot in which was *sopa de ajo con heuvos*.

'Dreaming about the blonde he met this morning,' Jaime, her husband, suggested.

Alvarez wondered at Jaime's capacity for saying the wrong thing at the wrong time. That Dolores had cooked so tasty a soup was proof she was once more in a good mood; should she believe he had been consorting with a young foreign woman and was in danger of losing his heart yet again, her mood would turn black quicker than an eyelid could blink. 'I'm dog-tired because I had to spend the morning listening to Salas talking so confusingly; I couldn't understand half of what he was saying.'

She added another half ladle of *sopas* to the plate in her hand, set this down in front of herself, sat. She tasted a spoonful. 'Should I have added a little more garlic?'

'Why try to improve on perfection?' Alvarez asked. If he had hoped his praise would divert her mind from what Jaime had said, he was mistaken.

'Where did you see Enrique this morning?' she asked.

'In the village,' Jaime answered.

'Why were you there?'

'Does a husband have to explain his every move?'

'Unless he wishes to be thought up to no good.'

'You think I maybe went along to the house with green shutters?'

'Why do you mention that place?' Her voice had become sharpened with ice.

'What are you getting at now? You can't think I would ever dream of going there?'

'A man's dreams are not fit for a woman of decency.'

'If you must know, I wasn't in the village and I didn't see Enrique.'

'You were lying?'

'It was a joke.'

'My mother often said that if a man admits to one lie, it is because he is trying to hide another two.'

'I wasn't within a couple of kilometres of the village until I came home.'

'She also said, "When a man denies something more than once, it is probably the truth."'

'Your mother . . .'

'Yes?'

'. . . didn't seem to like men,' he mumbled.

'She was a woman of much bitter experience.'

He reached across the table for the bottle of Bach.

'You have drunk too much already.'

'A man can drink what he wants in his own home.'

'And he can cook his own meals whether he wishes to or not.'

He withdrew his hand.

She turned to Alvarez. 'Why is the superior chief annoying you?'

He was grateful Jaime's admission had made it clear he had not been pursuing a young, nubile, foreign female. 'We've been asked to identify an Englishman who's arrived on the island after committing a large fraud at home . . .'

'How large?' Jaime interrupted.

'Half a million pounds.'

'What's that in euros or pesetas?'

'Something like seven hundred and fifty thousand euros.'

'There's one lucky man who can spend the rest of his life enjoying a big house, good wine, servants, a beautiful –' He stopped.

'Well?' Dolores asked sharply.

'Wife.'

'A man has to possess a fortune before he can have a beautiful wife?'

'Makes it a sight more likely.'

Was there no limit to Jaime's stupidity? Alvarez wondered. How could he lack the wit to have told her that their marriage proved the falsity of the question? Now, she'd lecture them on men's iniquities. To his surprise, she spoke peacefully.

'They say she has returned to the island to live in her inheritance.'

'Who's returned from where?' Jaime asked.

'You are so deep in wine, your mind is befogged?'

'I've only had a couple of glasses and how am I supposed to know who you're talking about when you don't name names.'

'Who has recently died, owning a grand *possessío*?'

'Old Eduardo.'

'Who was his nearest relative?'

'The niece who lives in France.'

'Since she married a Frenchman, naturally she is now divorced and so has no reason to stay there, much reason to return here. Had your mind not been absent, you would not have had to ask who I was talking about.'

'I'll bet Enrique couldn't work that out any more than I could.'

'Having just refilled his glass for the third time, that is quite likely.' Not concentrating on what she was doing, she picked up a small piece of bread and rubbed it into a pellet between forefinger and thumb. 'I was at school with Raquel. She was a complete liar . . .'

'You are admitting it is not only men who lie?'

'It is a pity you have never learned it is better to remain silent than to speak stupidity. She used to boast that her parents were wealthy, but they worked on the land and had no more pesetas than did our parents.' She dropped the pellet of bread, helped herself to another spoonful of *sopas*. 'She had mangy brown hair which she was stupid enough to try to grow into plaits. The boys pulled them and she would go and sneak to the teachers. We put some juice on her chair and she became embarrassed because she thought she had . . .'

'Had what?'

'It is not a memory for men's ears.'

'Then why tell it?'

'You have finished eating?'

'Yes.'

'Then you can clear the dirty plates and bring in the fruit that's on the kitchen table.'

Jaime was surprised and annoyed that he was being asked to do her job. But he for once exercised common sense and stood, collected up their plates, carried them through to the kitchen.

'Like I said,' Dolores continued, 'her parents were no richer than anyone else's, but she had an aunt with many pesetas because she had married a rich old man when she was only eighteen – by all accounts, the wedding sheets remained spotless. This aunt was always giving her chocolates, which is why she was so fat. She'd bring them to school to eat in front of us because it would make us envious since we could not afford such luxury. Enrique, why are people with much so often wicked?'

'To give those with little the chance to understand the benefits of having little to lose.'

'You are talking nonsense.'

Jaime pushed through the bead curtain, a bowl of fruit in one hand. He put the bowl down on the table, sat, helped himself to a pear.

Alvarez chose an apple. Dolores put a banana on her plate, did not immediately peel it. 'We called her monkey because she looked like one. She won't have changed.'

'Don't be so certain,' Alvarez remarked. 'I can remember Inés, who was nothing special when she was eleven, but by sixteen all the lads were galloping after her.'

'With you in the lead?' Jaime suggested.

'I'd met Juana-María by then,' he answered quietly. She had died, pinned against a wall by a drunken French driver. Alvarez still knew bitter sadness when he thought of her.

Dolores shared his sadness, as she shared the emotions of the others of her family. 'My mother used to say that life has to be endured, not enjoyed. Of course, she was referring to a woman's life, but it is occasionally the same for a man . . . Jaime, Enrique's glass is empty.'

'You're suggesting he has more wine instead of complaining he's drinking too much?' he asked in amazement.

She ignored him.

He picked up the bottle and reached across the table to refill Alvarez's glass, looked at her and noticed she was staring into space, then emptied the bottle into his own glass.

Four

As the last of the *policia* left the room, Alvarez congratulated himself. Each of them had a list of hotels, aparthotels, and letting agents whose staff he was to question; each person named was to be questioned and any possible identification of Faber referred to him. So the task facing him was far less onerous than it might have been. And in case anyone should accuse him of making others do his work, he had left himself with a hotel to visit.

Would the Englishman be identified? That was probably in the lap of the gods. The known facts suggested Faber had planned his crime with meticulous care and so it was reasonable to suppose he would have sensibly disguised himself – a few changes, even superficial ones if well executed, could hide a man except to a trained observer. There was always considerable difficulty in translating a written description into a visually recognizable face unless there was some unusual physical feature – a strangely shaped nose or mouth, rabbity ears, facial scars, advanced baldness. It seemed Faber was Mr Average-Looking Man.

His thoughts drifted. Time drifted. The phone rang to jerk his mind back to the present. 'Inspector Alvarez, Cuerpo General de Policia.'

'What are you doing there?'

It was Salas. 'Where, señor?'

'Are you incapable of understanding even the simplest question? I wish to know what you are doing there?'

'But where is there?'

'Where do you think?'

'I'm not certain.'

'You cannot tell me where you are at this moment?'

'Of course I can, señor.'

'Then will you kindly tell me?'

'But you must know since you phoned my office and I have answered.'

'Precisely.'

There was a long pause.

'Well?'

'I am not certain what you want, señor.'

'Goddamnit, I want you to tell me why you are in your office and not out on the streets, searching for the Englishman?'

'I have only a moment ago finished instructing the *policia* who are helping me in this monumental task. Naturally, I took the time to make them understand the necessity of not relying on the minutiae of the written description . . .'

'Why not?'

'If a description of you refers to your large nose—'

'You will not make insulting personal remarks.'

'If it refers to a large nose, a person has to remember that his conception of what the nose will look like may differ widely from the image in the mind of the person who gave the description. So that when a constable questions a man who has a nose which he regards as aquiline, he must not assume it is the same shape as that of the suspect, Faber.'

'There are those with sufficient common sense to know that without being told. Why did it take you over two hours to instruct the men?'

Alvarez looked at his watch. He was going to be late for his *merienda* at Club Llueso. 'Knowing the case must be solved efficiently in order to uphold the honour of the Cuerpo, I took great care they understood every word I spoke.'

'Asking for a miracle.'

'And then when they had gone and I was about to start my own enquiries, there was a phone call from a man who had committed suicide.'

'You are in communication with the dead?'

'Jorge frequently phones me in a state of great excitement and tells me he has killed himself and asks what he should do? He calms down when I explain that after committing suicide, the best thing to do is to go to the nearest bar and have a couple of *coñacs*.'

'Good God, man! since he's clearly mental, alcohol may well make his condition even worse.'

'He'll spend his day in a bar whatever I say. So my words give him some little comfort when he starts drinking.'

'Have you spoken to someone who would help him?'

'Only his wife could do that.'

'Then you have spoken to her?'

'No.'

'Why not?'

'He refuses to listen to anything she says.'

'I do wonder what the serious ailment was you so clearly suffered from when you were young. You tell me the only person who can help him is his wife, then that he scorns her.'

'He always listened to her – much more than most husbands listen to their wives – until she went off with a man from Mestara. It would not have upset him so much – she is a poor cook – had she chosen a man from Playa Neuva or Cala Roig.'

'How could that make any difference?'

'There has always been friendship with those two, but

bitter rivalry with Mestara. For instance, Lluesians always say Mestara women are *putas*; Mestara women say Lluesian men are limp. Which is nonsense. Jorge has become such a figure of fun because of his wife, he's asked how much she charges for a quickie.'

'A what?'

'A quickie.'

'What the devil is that?'

'A very brief . . . you know, señor.'

'I do not.'

'A skirts-up behind a wall.'

'If, unfortunately, I for once understand you, I am appalled. Even after all the years of exile on this island, I am appalled.' He slammed down the receiver.

There were more ways than one of shearing a sheep, Alvarez thought with satisfaction as he replaced the receiver. By introducing irrelevant misinformation with a sexual shading, bound to upset Salas's prudish soul, he had steered the conversation away from the problems of work and their solutions. He leaned over and opened the bottom right-hand drawer of the desk, brought out the bottle of Soberano and a glass. He was surprised to see how much brandy had been consumed.

Hotel Lunyamar was in a favoured position on the front in Port Llueso, separated from the beach by only a pedestrianized road. Since it catered mainly for English package tourists, the bar was the largest public room. Most meals were served buffet-style because trained waiters were becoming ever more expensive to hire, thanks to burgeoning welfare taxes as well as increased wages. The food was bland and chips were offered with everything but paella. There were always complaints about this omission.

Alvarez parked in front of a no-parking sign, walked

down the narrow road to the front. He stopped and stared out at the bay, as always rejoicing that he should live amidst such beauty. Could anywhere else possess such natural perfection as the oval, poster-blue bay and the majestic mountains which formed both ends?

He continued along to the hotel, stepped aside to allow a young woman in minimal bikini to come out. She smiled her thanks. Life, he thought sadly as he stepped into the foyer, was never fair. When he had been young, ladies, if sufficiently daring to go swimming where men were present, had worn costumes which left everything to the imagination.

Behind the reception desk, the assistant manager, Oreja, was talking to the receptionist. Oreja turned. 'Enrique! A long time since we last met.'

'Because I am having to work myself into an early grave,' Alvarez said, as they shook hands.

'You don't look quite ready to step in yet. Is the family well?'

'Thankfully, yes.'

'And the children?'

'Isabel gets very good grades for her work at school, but Juan doesn't seem to be able to improve on satisfactory. Dolores thinks he'll end up sweeping the streets.'

'By the time he needs a job, that'll be very well paid because no one will want to do it.'

A woman to Alvarez's right spoke in a loud, harsh voice. She was, to be polite, well built; her hairstyle, make-up, and dress might have suited a woman half her age. 'Is anyone going to serve me?' she demanded in English.

'The receptionists are rather busy, dear, dealing with other guests,' said her husband.

'I am not standing here all morning.'

'There's always at least one like her in every busload,'

Oreja said in Mallorquin, confident that she would, even if listening, not understand a word.

'Service in this hotel is abysmal!' she announced.

'Yes, dear.'

'The food is a disgrace. What was that mess last night?'

'Stuffed aubergines.'

'And the one they called a speciality?'

'The waiter said it was typical Mallorquin and we should try it . . .'

'The staff should not be familiar.'

'I think he was only trying to help.'

'One does not seek the help of a waiter.'

'Fred told me he ate the speciality and it was delicious.'

'You cannot expect someone of his ilk to have an educated palate.'

Alvarez said in Mallorquin, 'She's going to cause trouble.'

'You think she's been doing anything else since she arrived?'

'I need some information.'

'Then let's get out of earshot.'

To the left behind the reception desk was a small office; the untidy clutter of papers, files and books bore witness to the pressures of Oreja's work.

'I presume it's not too early to offer you a drink?' Oreja said.

'Soon, it would become too late.'

He smiled. 'What would you like?'

'*Coñac* with just ice.'

Oreja left the room; he returned, sat on the swivel chair in front of the old, battered desk. 'So what would you like to know? Does the young lady with long black hair sleep in thirty-three?'

'The names of Englishmen who have arrived here on or after the nineteenth.'

'Why do you want to know that?'

'I have to try to identify someone whose close relative urgently needs to get in touch with him.'

'And the relative hasn't considered lifting a receiver and dialling?'

'Not everyone is as intelligent as you.'

'And few are as duplicitous as you. Nevertheless, as a good citizen I accept your explanation without believing a word of it and will ask Adolfo to provide the information. Won't be a moment.' He left.

Oreja might enjoy a good salary, Alvarez judged, but his life was one long hassle. Suppliers failed to deliver on time; essential equipment broke down; rooms became overbooked; delayed flights meant guests arriving in the middle of the night after the staff had exercised their right to leave at the end of their working day; guests complained while enjoying a lifestyle well beyond that of their own homes. Perhaps his work in the Cuerpo was not quite as exhausting as he had always held it to be . . .

Oreja returned, accompanied by a waiter. The waiter passed one glass to Alvarez, in which was a measure of brandy that even he considered generous, another to Oreja, then left.

'You once told me you'd like to quit the Cuerpo. But it's not happened?' Oreja said.

'Every week, I buy a *decimo* in the lottery and dream. Every week, the dream vanishes as I tear up the ticket and swear never to waste good money again.'

'If I won a few million pesetas . . . It's odd how I still think in pesetas when I'm dealing with those damned euros all the time.'

'Not even a government can wash away a lifetime's habit.'

'Yet they try . . . If I win a fortune, I'll drive to Palma, book in at one of the two top hotels, and complain about everything. Or maybe I'll stay at both, one after the other.'

'You're fortunate to have such a chance. If I made a nuisance of myself in the Cuerpo, I'd be arrested.'

After a brief silence, Alvarez said, 'I'd better think of moving, so what about the names?'

'Miguel is drawing up a list . . . It's unlike you to be in a rush.'

'The superior chief expects me to work twenty-five hours a day. A Madrileño.'

'Like one of our directors. An arrogant bastard.'

There was a knock on the door and one of the waiters entered, handed a sheet of paper to Oreja. He was about to leave when Oreja stopped him. 'Enrique, do you have to leave immediately?'

'Not quite that quickly.'

'When two friends meet after a long time, two drinks are a minimum.' He spoke to the waiter. 'A *coñac* for the inspector and a fino for me.' The waiter left. 'Now, Enrique, you've mentioned the children. Tell me more about Jaime and Dolores.'

'They're very fit.'

'And she continues to speak her mind?'

'Frequently.'

'She has many strong views. How times have changed! Women with strong views used to keep them to themselves; these days they are even in the government. Belén was right when he said, "Life is change, most of it unwelcome" . . . Here's the list.' He passed it across.

There were fourteen names. 'What can you tell me about these people?' Alvarez asked.

'Nothing unless I've had reason to meet or hear about them.'

'Meyer?'

'A blank.'

'Heane?'

'The same.'

'Lodge?'

'Disabled and his wife has to push him around in a wheelchair. Always polite and smiling, whereas others who are fit are rude and sour. It often does seem that adversity brings out the best in one.'

'I'd rather not find out. What about Wheelan?'

'You've seen him. The man with the complaining wife.'

A name to be crossed off, Alvarez thought. A man willing to suffer her would lack the courage to steal a bar of chocolate from a supermarket. He read out the remaining names; Oreja could tell him nothing about them. Thirteen who had to be visually identified. Common sense said he should pass some of these names on to the *policia* who were helping him, leaving him the better to co-ordinate.

The waiter was taking a long time to return with their drinks. Perhaps the vocal lady was correct and the service was poor.

Alvarez was contemplating life and supper when Montalavo entered the room.

'Four names I've followed up.' Montalavo put a sheet of paper down on the desk.

'You've only managed four?'

'You reckon it's easy to get names and then find the person. Time and again I couldn't nail the man because he was somewhere on the beach, chasing women, lucky sod. Maybe you think you could have done better?'

'Probably.'

'I'd really like to see that.' Montalavo brought a notebook out of his pocket, opened it. 'Noyes, Mindon and Stanton-Ayes . . . Funny names the English have . . . You can forget. Noyes wouldn't make a metre-fifty if he stood on tip-toe; Minter is seventy years plus; Stanton-Ayes has a noticeable scar on his right cheek; but Mercer could be a possible.' He moved a chair away from the wall and sat. 'Unlike you, I haven't been sitting on my backside all day and my legs are tired . . . Steven Mercer arrived on the twentieth. Age, build, colour of eyes, and so on, could match. More to the point, the moment he learned who I was, he became nervous. I've a gut feeling about him.'

'How did you explain the reason for talking to him?'

'Like you said, of course.'

'Is he on his own?'

'A woman let me in – a bit of all right – and I heard another man's voice. Mercer told me they're a couple who work for the letting agency and clean up the house and garden.'

'Where is this?'

'Villa Bellavista, on the back road from here to Playa Neuva; past the *torrente* and on the right-hand side. A house with brownish shutters and a palm tree slap in front of it. He's here for three months, writing a book.'

'What about?'

'How the hell would I know? But I can tell you something: he'll be paying a rent and a half. My wife's cousin has a place on the front at Cala Baston and gets five hundred euros a week in the season – black, of course. I can remember when no one paid a hundred pesetas a month unless he was crazy or a foreigner.'

'And a man could afford to buy a house.'

'If he'd the sense. Years ago, the place next to my parents' house was up for sale. My father wanted to buy it; my mother said the owner was being too greedy. He listened to her and didn't buy. Now it's worth God knows how many times more.'

'It doesn't do to look back.'

'Or forward. There was a programme about an asteroid hitting the earth and killing everyone. So when my wife said we couldn't afford a new CD player, I told her, "If we don't buy it and are killed off tomorrow by an asteroid, we'll have wasted all the money we haven't spent." '

'So you bought it?'

'You're not married . . . I'm off home, then.'

'You've time to track down another name.'

'You reckon I've nothing better to do than work?'

Montalavo was right: work diminished a man's life. If he did not have to work, he could buy a finca (How? These days one had to be a millionaire to buy a finca) and grow fruit and vegetables, have a large flock of red sheep which were peculiar to the island and help to prevent the tragedy of their extinction.

It was time to return home. What would Dolores be cooking? Might she be in an extravagant mood and preparing *chuletas de cordero al sarmiento*? Even to think of the small lamb chops grilled over vine shoots was to make the mouth water . . . Yet as Montalavo had suggested, it didn't do to look forward because that could so easily lead to bitter frustration. Dolores might once more be in a bad mood and deliberately preparing a meal which he would hasten to forget.

The phone rang. He did not lift the receiver since it was unlikely Salas would want to talk to him this late in the evening. It stopped ringing. Many of life's irritations could be dismissed by ignoring them. It began to ring again and he swore. Mallorquin was a satisfying language in which to express resentment as it plumbed the depths of blasphemous vulgarity.

'Is that the Cuerpo General de Policia,' a woman asked excitedly.

'Yes.'

'There's been a robbery – a very big robbery. Someone broke into the house and—'

'Who's speaking?'

'Margarita Beccaría. Doña Rexach went up to her bedroom and found her jewellery was gone.'

'Where are you speaking from?'

'Sa Echona.'

The *possessió* which some woman who had been at school with Dolores had inherited. He silently swore again. This was likely to be trouble. The wealthy always created far more trouble for the police than the ordinary person. They seemed to feel betrayed because wealth should insulate them from the problems of life.

'Are you still there?'

'I was waiting for you to tell me more.'

'What more is there to say?'

'When was the theft?'

'Who can know? Doña Rexach went up to her bedroom and found the jewellery missing.'

'Is the method of ingress obvious?'

'How do you mean?'

'Is there a window in the bedroom broken?'

'I don't know. She just said to tell you to come immediately.'

Do that and he would not return home in time to enjoy a drink or two before the meal. The theft was over and done with and nothing he could do or say would alter that fact. 'I'll be along as soon as possible.'

'You've got to come now.'

'Your problem is not the only trouble I have to which I must give my expert attention. The loss of jewellery cannot have priority over the need to find a missing daughter.'

'But—'

'Can you not imagine the suffering of the mother? Her mind will be flooded with nightmares of what might have happened to her daughter.'

'Of course you must do everything to find the girl. It's

just that Doña Rexach can be very annoyed when things don't happen as she wants them to.'

'She would have me abandon my search for the girl and worry about her jewellery instead, when that will be insured so that she will suffer no loss?'

'I will explain to her.'

'You can add that much police work is carried out unseen. While I cannot visit Sa Echona immediately, I will somehow find time to speak to a man whose ears are tuned to crimes committed in the area. He may know who is the thief and if the jewels are yet being offered for sale.'

'I'll say you'll be here first thing in the morning.'

'I will arrive as soon as possible.' He said goodbye, rang off. A quick look at his watch showed he had not been delayed for as long as he feared.

Five

When Alvarez walked through the *entrada* – spotlessly clean to prove Dolores was a good housewife – into the sitting/dining room, Isabel and Juan were arguing; as he sat at the table and reached for the bottle of Soberano, Juan called his sister a name still normally restricted to all-male company.

Dolores pushed through the bead curtain, a wooden spoon in her hand, a flour-smudged apron over her colourful dress. 'Who said that?'

'Said what?' Jaime asked.

'You did not hear your son call his sister a word from the gutter? Shall I tell you why? It is because you so often speak as he did.'

'That's not fair.'

'You do not speak in front of the children words that make a woman blush?'

'Maybe I swear occasionally, but I don't say anything which isn't on television, so they've heard it all often enough.'

'For you, repetition, far from exacerbating filth, cleanses it?'

Alvarez emptied his glass. Why could Jaime not understand that a contented wife was one whose husband did not argue with her? Soon, Dolores would be in such a bad mood that they would dine on chick peas. He sent a mental message to Jaime to shut up. It failed to arrive.

'What I'm saying is, I'm not teaching them anything new.'

'You are teaching them that filth is acceptable. My mother was not wrong when she said a man with peasant tastes can never hide them.'

'She worked in the fields, same as my mother did.'

'An aristocrat can till the land, yet remain an aristocrat; a tramp can live in a palace, yet remain a tramp.'

'What the hell have tramps and aristocrats to do with anything?' He picked up his glass, found it was empty, reached for the bottle of brandy.

'You have had enough,' Dolores snapped.

'I know when I've had enough.'

'There are many things you do not know and that is one of them.' She sighed. 'I suppose I must return and finish cooking. I wonder why I slave for hour after hour in a kitchen as hot as the fires which burn martyrs when my work is not noticed, let alone appreciated?' She swept the wooden spoon through the air as if attacking a recalcitrant batter. 'Men can appreciate only themselves. They expect to be waited on from morning to night and have no regard for those who do the waiting. Aiyee! We women are today's victims.' She turned and swept through the bead curtain into the kitchen.

Jaime, as silently as possible, poured himself another drink. 'Sometimes she talks like . . . like she's crazy.'

Juan called out, 'Mama, Papa says you are crazy.'

Jaime swore.

Dolores put her head through the bead curtain. 'Perhaps he speaks more truly than he can realize since I continue to work to please him, knowing he is indifferent to all the sacrifices I make.' She withdrew.

'Why does she get herself in such a state?' Jaime asked.

The meal was neither the one of Alvarez's imagination, nor the disaster he had feared. The *pollo a la Catalana* would not have disgraced a three-star restaurant. The *picada* of ground toasted almonds, bread sautéed in olive oil, pine nuts and chicken tasted little short of ambrosia.

Alvarez was peeling a banana when he said to Dolores, 'I'll be meeting an old friend of yours tomorrow.'

'Who?'

'Doña Rexach.'

She held the segment of orange in front of her mouth. 'Good God!'

'You shouldn't speak like that in front of the children,' Jaime said sanctimoniously.

She turned to face Alvarez. 'Why are you seeing her?'

'Her jewellery has been stolen.'

'Then the thief has helped himself to a fortune. The moment she learned of her uncle's death, she will have emptied many a jeweller's shop. She will have worn far too many jewels in order to look with contempt at those who wear none.'

'Poor woman!'

'You talk as stupidly as my husband.'

'You are so rude about her.'

'I am no such thing.'

'Haven't you just said she'll have bought jewellery merely to boast?'

'That is fact, not rudeness.'

Dolores had called him three times, ever more loudly, before he found the will to get out of bed. To hurry was to risk mistake, so he did not rush his dressing or his breakfast of two slices of *coca* and a cupful of hot chocolate. When he left home and settled in his Ibiza, parked close to the front door, he did not drive off immediately, but considered an immediate problem: should he drive straight to Villa Bellavista? Or should he fulfil his promise to Margarita to go to Sa Echona first? If he spent time at Sa

Echona, he would not be furthering his investigation into the possible whereabouts of Faber and Salas would refuse to listen to excuses. If he did not go to Sa Echona, Doña Rexach would complain bitterly. Whose anger was to be the more respected?

Villa Bellavista lay just beyond a flat-topped hill, on the road to Playa Neuva, three kilometres from Llueso. Originally a small, primitive rock-built house, it had been reformed and enlarged by a Mallorquin who had not bothered about building permission because his brother was on the local council. In the garden was a tall, ancient palm tree whose trunk had been skilfully smoothed, a lawn recently mown, and a single flower bed filled with roses in which not a single weed was visible. Clearly the gardener was more conscientious than many who were employed to look after rented property – one of the numerous jobs unknown before the advent of tourism. Beyond and to the right of the house, the corner of a swimming pool was visible; the water glinted as the very light wind disturbed its surface.

When he rang the bell, the door was opened by a young woman. The nature of his job demanded he closely studied those he met. She was to be admired for her soft brown hair with highlights, her deep-brown eyes, retroussé nose, generous mouth, dimpled chin, swan-like neck, and, above all, that extra something – impossible to define – which assured a man that when conditions were right, she welcomed passion. Her dress had a generous décolletage and, without doing so blatantly, outlined a shapely body. Sadly, she wore engagement and wedding rings. Montalavo had been quite correct: she was an attractive dish. 'Is Señor Mercer here?' he asked in English.

'Yes, he is?' she answered, her voice rising to make it a question.

'I'd like to talk to him.'

'Your name, please?'

'Inspector Alvarez of the Cuerpo General de Policia.'

'Another policeman! Is something more wrong?'

'We are still trying to find the lady who is needed back in England. I have to know if Señor Mercer has remarked anything which may help.'

'Come on in.'

He followed her through a small *entrada* and into an oblong sitting room which had been furnished without taste or quality. Sunlight came through the large picture window and gave the dull room bright life.

He watched her leave. At each step, the frock briefly tightened to reveal the curve of a neat buttock.

A couple of minutes later, Mercer entered. 'Susan tells me you're another policeman?'

'Inspector Alvarez, of the Cuerpo General de Policia,' he said for the second time.

'What kind of policeman does that make you? . . . No offence meant.' He chuckled.

'A detective, señor.' The other's age, height, build, colouring, hairstyle, shape of ears and nose, were roughly within the boundaries of the written description of Faber. And, as Montalavo had remarked, he appeared to be nervous.

'Susan said you're asking about the woman again?'

'That is correct.'

'I told the policeman yesterday I was afraid I couldn't help.'

'I know, señor, but we find that a person sometimes remembers something fresh if he's asked questions a second time. I'm hoping you'll be kind enough to answer them again.'

'Of course, but I assure you there's nothing to remember . . . Would you like some coffee?'

'Thank you.'

'I've learned it is the custom to have a brandy with morning coffee. Will you join me or do you have to say no to the brandy because you're working?'

'I try never to offend custom, señor.'

'Wise man. I'll ask Susan or Dick to lay it on. If you'll excuse me?' He left.

A possible, Alvarez thought, but his immediate impression was that Mercer lacked the inner strength to steal half a million pounds. But then, of course, the scent of money could make a rat out of a mouse.

Mercer returned. 'It'll be along in a moment.' He sat.

'You are on holiday, señor?'

'A working holiday.'

'I am not certain what that means.'

'I'm a would-be author; always wanted to write, never had time to try more than short stories which ended in the wastepaper basket. Then my godfather died and I inherited; his wife had predeceased him and he was my uncle as well as godfather. There was enough money to quit my job and come out here – having visited the island on holiday, I knew how lovely it was if one kept away from the concrete jungles. I hoped that inspiration would flourish, but so far it hasn't begun to shoot. I think I may be the first writer to suffer writer's block before the first chapter's written.'

'What did you do in England which you happily gave up?'

'I worked in a small agricultural firm.'

'A considerable change to writing!'

Susan entered with a tray. She held this for Alvarez to help himself to sugar and milk; because she was leaning forward, he was not concentrating on what he was doing and inadvertently emptied a spoonful of sugar half into the cup, half on to the saucer.

She put a glass down on the small table by his side, straightened up, crossed to the chair where Mercer sat.

'Thanks, Susan,' he said.

'What about lunch?'

'I suppose I must keep my nose to the grindstone even if that's not turning. I'll have it here.'

'And supper?'

'I'll try that restaurant you mentioned.'

'The *lomo con col* is really good.'

'I'll report on it tomorrow morning.'

She smiled, turned, left the room.

'I'm very lucky,' Mercer said.

'To be on the island?' Alvarez suggested.

'That, of course, but I was thinking of Susan and her husband. She looks after me as if I weren't just another tourist and he's ready to give a hand any time, even though he's more than enough work with all the gardens and pools to keep in trim.' He raised his glass. 'Your health.'

'And yours, señor.' Alvarez drank. One of the better brandies. Money made certain that even if all people were born equal, they didn't live equally. 'Señor, as you know, we are trying to find an English woman who is here on holiday and whose close relative is seriously ill. Unfortunately, all that is known is that she is staying in, or near, Port Llueso. So we are asking as many tourists as possible if they have seen her. She must be a fairly striking woman because her hair is dyed a bright orange. You may have seen someone with orange hair when you have walked around the port or the village.'

'As I told your colleague, I haven't, because I spend so much of my time staring at the typewriter. Conscience may make cowards of others; it tries to stop me turning into a slacker.'

'You do not go out in the evening?'

'Sometimes. But the frustration of being thwarted makes

me very lackadaisical. But when I have wandered around, I haven't seen anyone with orange hair. And I certainly would have noticed her if I had because I've never understood how women can be so indifferent to other people's sensibilities as to dye their hair that sort of colour.'

'It was a hope you would have noticed her.'

'Sadly, unfulfilled . . . Look, excuse me a moment.' He stood. 'I want a word with Dick.' He crossed to the French windows, opened them, went out and walked to the pool. A man who had been cleaning the surface of the water held the scoop upright as Mercer walked up to him. He nodded, put the pole down and, as Mercer returned into the sitting room, limped away. Black hair, beginning to bald, designer stubble – too lazy to shave? – Alvarez automatically noted; he felt his own chin to make certain he had shaved that morning.

Mercer returned and sat. 'Keeps the pool crystal-clear and the garden spick and span. The letting people said that they were a first-class couple.'

'He has been injured?'

'Some months before he came out here he had a nasty bike crash. And if that wasn't enough, the firm for which he was working made him and a load of others redundant. Susan, who has all the push, told me he became more and more depressed until she decided they'd try to find a new life. The letting agents took them on in September, last year, and say they've never regretted doing so.'

'Who are the agents?'

'Morgan and Gaya. I'm told there's never been a Morgan, but an English name encourages punters.'

Susan entered with two glasses. When she put one down on the table by his side, Alvarez was careful to look away.

Back at the office there were two reports on Alvarez's desk. Rotger had spoken to Mallett, Parr and Dunn. None of them could be Faber. He felt relieved. The case could have developed into one surpassing the labours of Hercules; now, it was only going to be too much hard and unwanted work.

The phone rang. 'The superior chief will speak to you,' the secretary said.

He stared at the far wall and wondered why men like Salas lived.

'Alvarez?'

'Yes, señor.'

'Have you identified the Englishman?'

'Not yet.'

'Why not?'

'It is an impossible task . . .'

'The Cuerpo does not recognize the word "impossible". And had you the ability to conduct a case efficiently, no doubt it would be completed by now.'

'The problem of identifying a newly arrived Englishman in his forties amongst the horde of tourists is a daunting one . . .'

'You have no one helping you?'

'Yes, but—'

'You have more buts than a goat.'

Alvarez was astonished by this irrelevant remark from someone normally so boringly prosaic. 'The trouble is that Englishmen of that age spend their days on the beaches and their nights in discothèques. That makes it extremely difficult to meet them . . .

'Why presume they spend their time so wastefully?'

'It's in their nature to cruise.'

'You have a problem? One moment you tell me the English are on the beaches or in discothèques, the next that they're at sea.'

The superior chief was all at sea. 'Not that kind of cruising, señor.'

'What other kind is there?'

'The other.'

'You are quite incomprehensible.'

'He is a man in his forties. What does a man of his age do in his spare time?'

'One hopes something useful or mind-enhancing.'

'It is more likely he looks for a woman or, in the case of someone like Faber, a man.'

There was a long silence before Salas said, 'Could even a psychiatrist understand your desire to introduce perverted matters into every conversation?'

'I am trying to explain why it is so difficult to identify the men we need to question.'

'So difficult that you have, as usual, made no progress.'

'That is not quite true because—'

'Let me assure you that you have not once conducted a case with the competence expected of an officer of the Cuerpo.'

'I was trying to explain that it's not true I have made no progress. There is a possible identification. A man called Mercer. Both a *policia* and I have gained the impression that talking to him makes him nervous.'

'In your case, more likely uncomprehending. How closely does he fit the description of Faber?'

'Quite closely. Which does raise the question: would he not have made some effort to adopt a working measure of disguise?'

'Did you not read the report from England?'

'Of course, señor.'

'Yet it has escaped you that the English police are convinced he will believe no one can possibly know to where he has fled. In these circumstances, is he likely to bother to try to alter his appearance when there has to be the possibility, however faint, the alteration might be noted and commented upon?'

'Perhaps this lack of such effort is a further disguise. By that, I mean . . .'

'Do you intend to question him closely?'

'Not just yet.'

'The thought of conducting this case expeditiously escapes you?'

'I have always believed it is best not to approach a suspect head-on until one has facts to challenge what he says. If I have a word with the couple who look after the place he's renting, perhaps they'll tell me something I know is important but will have no significance to them.'

'An intelligent officer should not rely on presumptions. You will speak to this couple immediately and then question Mercer. Is that clear?'

'Yes, señor.'

Alvarez replaced the receiver. He checked the time: a quarter past twelve. Before too long he could return home for lunch. The door opened and one of the *policia* – he couldn't remember the other's name – entered and placed a sheet of paper on the desk. 'That's my lot finished.'

As the other left, Alvarez picked up the paper. He had hoped for a clear negative, but out of four men one had to be considered. Multiply that out . . . He'd originally feared the worst, then had gained the relief of thinking he might have no more than a couple of suspects at the most. Now . . .

Perhaps it was pessimism that caused him to park outside the offices of Morgan and Gaya instead of driving straight home; emotions could cause one to behave out of character.

Behind the single show window were numerous cards advertising houses to rent and a couple for sale, at prices almost impossible to believe were serious. If, he thought as he entered, he had had the sense (and capital) to buy half a dozen broken-down fincas even forty years before, he would now have been a millionaire. But he had been born to be poor. And overworked.

The young lady behind the large table which acted as an informal counter was smartly dressed and sharply made-up. She received him with disinterest, correctly identifying his purchasing ability.

'Inspector Alvarez, Cuerpo,' he said. 'I want a word with the boss.'

'Why?'

'I'll explain to him.'

She was annoyed. She turned and went into the office beyond the far side of the table and closed the door behind herself with unnecessary force. There were three easy chairs – prospective customers must be soothed – and he sat on one. He stared at a large vase of mixed flowers, then at a painting of the bay – as if any painting could do justice to that beauty. Years before there had not been an estate agent in the village or the port; now there were several, a tribute to the very high commission charged.

The assistant returned. 'In there.' She nodded her head at the open doorway, then ignored him.

'Fernando Antignac,' the manager said as he came round the large desk and shook hands.

Full of friendliness. Not a man from whom to buy a second-hand house.

'Please sit.'

He sat.

'How can I help you? There's no problem with our work, I trust?'

A touch of worry? Rather too much black money around when a member of the Cuerpo called? 'I'm just after some information.'

Antignac relaxed. 'I'll be happy to give you all I can. I imagine it is not to do with the cost of buying or renting a house for yourself.'

Sarcastic sod, Alvarez thought. 'You employ staff to look after the properties.'

'Women to clean and, if the client wishes, to cook; men to keep the pools clean and the gardens tidy.'

'You have an English couple called Thorne.'

'No problem with them, I hope?'

'None that I know of.'

'Good. It's difficult to find staff as conscientious as they. But still you are interested in them?'

'Only because of something that it is just possible they could help us with. How and when did they start with you?'

'Walked in one day and she asked if we could give them work. Dick said he'd been keen on gardening in England and Susan claimed to be a good cook. Wasn't certain he'd be much good with his leg injury, but it's difficult to get reliable employees these days so we took them on trial. They were as good as they'd claimed – his work was as sharp as hers – so they've stayed with us.'

'When did you first employ them?'

'It was last year, maybe September, because that's when we had to fire someone; but I'd have to check the records to make certain.'

'That doesn't matter. Have they been with you since then?'

'We kept them on during the winter; to tell the truth, if we'd let them go as is usual with foreigners, we might have lost them for this year. In fact it paid off because there was more winter letting than usual.'

Alvarez stood. 'Thanks for your help.' He left. It had occured to him at the house that Thorne's facial features and build came within the written description of Faber sent from England. And hair could be died, baldness induced, a limp faked. But Thorne was married. He was having to work. And no one could be in two places at the same time.

Six

Alvarez and Jaime were enjoying a drink when the telephone rang. After the sixth ring, Dolores came through the bead curtain from the kitchen. 'It has not occurred to either of you to answer since you have nothing to do but drink while I have all the washing-up?'

It hadn't.

'The longer a man lives, the deafer he becomes until a cork is drawn.' She hurried through to the *entrada*.

'It's all America's fault,' Jaime said. 'Making women believe men should do work about the house. My mother would never have expected my father to answer the phone.'

'Because they hadn't one?'

'That's right, try to be smart . . . but it's like all that fast food. Women buy it because they can sit down and watch the telly, instead of taking the time to cook.'

'It's the way of modern life.'

'It's women's laziness.'

Dolores returned to the sitting room. 'The arrogant bitch!' She continued on through the bead curtain into the kitchen.

They stared at the strings of beads swinging into each other with diminishing momentum. 'She swore!' Jaime finally said, his voice pitched high from astonishment.

'Is swearing solely a masculine pleasure?' she demanded as she reappeared in the doorway, an empty saucepan in her right hand, a trail of beads over her left shoulder.

'But look how you go on at me if I swear.'

'Your swearing is crude and unnecessary. Should I swear, I do so with taste and for good cause. How can that bitch believe that just because she is wealthy I'll kneel to her? I don't kneel to anyone, least of all an arrogant *puta* like her.' She swished the saucepan through the air.

'Who phoned?' Alvarez asked.

'Is there anyone else so condescendingly insulting? When she learned who I was, she invited us to a meal!'

'Surely that's a friendly gesture from whoever it was?'

'You believe Raquel Rexach would ask us to her castle for dinner if not to pour Vega Sicilia, knowing we drink only *vino corriente*, to serve the largest prawns, because we have to content ourselves with salted cod, the finest *solomillo*, because we can only afford scrag-end?'

'If that sort of a meal is on offer, I bet you accepted even if she is a bitch,' Jaime said.

She stared at her husband. 'My mother often remarked that a man's soul resides in his belly.' She turned, stamped her way back into the kitchen.

Jaime refilled his glass. 'Why turn down a really good meal?'

'Because she's convinced we were being asked for malicious reasons.'

'How can she think so daft?'

'Don't you remember her telling us she was at school with this Raquel woman and they couldn't stand each other?'

'She's going on about what happened all those years ago?'

'Women seldom forgive and never forget.'

'You know, that's dead right! She went for me all ends up not so long ago because I forgot something or other. Yet when she forgets something, I always forgive her . . .'

'I have done something wrong which needs your

forgiveness?' Dolores demanded, as she reappeared, without a saucepan.

Jaime mumbled.

'What's that?' She waited, then addressed Alvarez: 'I have to confess, I was misguided enough to hope you had a little respect for me.'

'There's no one I respect more,' he hastened to assure her.

'Yet you provide her with reason to believe my family is thoughtless and feckless.'

'What on earth are you talking about?'

'Have I not explained why she phoned?'

'No, you haven't.'

'Men hear only what they wish to hear. As I said only one moment ago, Raquel rang because the post has given her your home number.'

'They're forbidden to do that and you didn't say why she phoned.'

'Wine has clouded your mind completely. She complained because you had not arrived at her castle as you'd promised.'

'I forgot because of what else was happening. Shit!'

'You will not speak such language in this house. Whilst she is a person one naturally wishes to forget, your forgetfulness will, now she knows you are my cousin, have afforded her great pleasure, since it shows your word is not to be relied upon. She demands you go there immediately. She plainly believes she has only to speak for you to run. So you will go nowhere until after a long siesta.' She returned to the kitchen.

'I never know what she's going to do or say,' Jaime remarked plaintively.

Alvarez drank. 'She's a woman,' he said, as he put the empty glass down on the table.

* * *

Sa Echona was the classical mansion of a *possessió*. Built around an inner courtyard access to which was through an arched entrance, its walls, four floors high, were of rock, expertly shaped by men for whom time had been of little consequence. Beyond this were less imposing, much smaller buildings in which servants and farm hands had lived, oil had been pressed from gathered olives, horses and mules had been housed, crops stored. Once, the undulating land to the mountains had belonged to the estate.

Alvarez climbed out of his car and studied the house. It was poorly proportioned and without architectural grace, yet it possessed the strength of permanence. It had been built two hundred and fifty years before, would be there in two hundred and fifty years' time. What modern building could claim even half such a future.

He crossed the gravel drive and climbed the five steps to the large portico. He did not immediately press the bell to the side of the thick, heavy, panelled wooden door. Even if she was half the formidable woman Dolores described, he was in for a rough time. He should have ignored Dolores's demand that he enjoy a long siesta, remembered that riches meant power and driven here immediately after she had rung. If she complained, Salas would accept her version of events without bothering to listen to anything he said.

He reluctantly pressed the bell. The door was swung back, with much metallic screeching from the ancient hinges, by a middle-aged woman. 'I should like to speak to Doña Rexach.'

'And you are . . .?'

Her speech told him she came from Mestara. She was so neatly dressed that as he announced who he was, he remembered he had been wearing his shirt for rather a long time.

He was shown into a large room, its contents half-hidden

in the gloom of closed shutters. When she opened these, the room became a monument to the past. Framed photographs of elderly men and women hung on the walls, a pair of flintlock guns were crossed above the large, elaborate marble mantelpiece. The four chairs with needlework seats had the straight-backed, uncomfortable form popular in the nineteenth century; the angular settee was covered in a funereal material; the piano had an ancient music stand for two musicians; the leather of the adjustable dual stool was cracked. He studied the photographs. The women looked stern and highly moral; doubtless Raquel inherited her nature from them. The men possessed the self-importance that wealth provided . . . He heard approaching footsteps, turned to face the doorway.

She was not beautiful – too near middle age for that – but she did possess attractive features. Her light-brown hair was styled without fuss; she used some make-up, but this with careful frugality; her colourful, patterned frock looked simple, but graceful. 'Good evening.'

'Good evening, Doña Rexach.'

'Thank you for coming here.'

'It is no problem.'

'Your name is?'

'Inspector Alvarez . . .'

'Margarita told me that. I'm asking for your Christian name.'

'Enrique.'

'Shall we go through, Enrique?'

Monkey-faced and bitchy? First acquaintance denied both.

The large south-facing room had modern furniture and was filled with light and colour.

'Please sit.'

He settled on a chair of luxurious quality.

'May I offer you a drink?'

'That would be very acceptable.'

She crossed to the far wall and pressed a bell, returned to sit opposite him. 'Have you found the girl? I've been worrying about her all the time.'

He wondered whom she was talking about.

Margarita stepped into the room.

'Would you get us some drinks? I'll have a fino and the inspector will tell you what he would like.'

'*Coñac*, please,' he said, 'with just ice.'

Margarita left.

'Am I silly to hope that since you don't appear to be very disturbed, she has been found?'

He finally remembered telling Margarita over the phone why he could not drive out to Sa Echona the previous night. 'Thankfully, that is so.'

'What had happened to her?'

What did a young girl do? She met with friends and lost all account of time. 'She met with some friends and lost all account of time.'

'Thank goodness it was nothing serious. I hope her mother has made her well aware of all the distress she's caused others. And all the extra work for you.'

'When a young person is missing, it is not work to try and find her.'

'I'm delighted to hear you say that. Dolores must be very proud of you and the work you do. But I do wonder if she shows that. As I remember, she was always . . . not inclined to reveal her more tender moments. I had hoped she'd come here and we would enjoy meeting again, but she didn't seem to think that possible. Do you know why?'

'I'm afraid not.'

Margarita returned with two glasses on a silver salver, handed one to him, one to Raquel. The brandy was of superior quality, but for once his mind was not on what he was drinking. How was he going to explain his failing to turn up immediately to investigate the robbery? At the moment, remarkably, she was in a pleasant mood, but that could change in a second. He drank deeply, said: 'I should like to—'

'I'm sorry, but I must say something first.'

He braced himself.

'I spoke to someone at the *guardia* post to ask for your home number because I had to speak to you. He was very reluctant to give it to me.'

Not reluctant enough.

'I realize . . . I don't know quite how to explain.'

Nor did he.

'I can't think how I could have been so silly. I suppose I hid them before I went to Palma because I'd heard there had been one or two recent burglaries and I decided the safe was far too old to be trusted; the new one's ordered, but not yet installed. I must admit that when Margarita said you couldn't come here, I was rather annoyed, but thank goodness you couldn't since . . . Well, last night, I remembered where I'd put the jewellery.'

Did he dare believe he had heard correctly? 'You have not had it stolen?'

'I was tempted just to ring and tell you. But that would have been rather cowardly, so I asked you to come here in order to apologize personally. Margarita said you would speak to a man who might know who had stolen the jewellery. Will you have to tell him how stupid I've been?'

'There'll be no need to say anything.'

'You're being so kind, especially considering all the worry and work I've caused you.'

'That's of small account when I know you have not lost anything.'

She drank slowly, put the glass down. 'You were going to say something when I interrupted you. You would like to what?'

It would be ridiculous to apologize for his negligence now there was no need to do so. 'I'm sorry, but I've forgotten.'

'Then tell me how Dolores is, what family she has and how they are.'

Three-quarters of an hour later, he prepared to leave, after having enjoyed a second brandy.

'Enrique, you must let me give form to my thanks and prove I am not normally half-witted. Come here and have a meal.'

If Dolores's jealousy was a guide, it would be a meal to remember. Starting with prawns the size of small lobsters? 'It would be a pleasure.'

'Luncheon or dinner?'

'Dinner would be better because I never know what's happening with work during the day.'

'Dinner it shall be. Will you name an evening?'

'How about Monday?'

'I'm almost certain that will be fine, but I'll just check.' She stood, crossed to a small desk, picked up and opened an appointments book. 'Monday evening it is.' She made an entry, shut the book, replaced it. 'I suppose Dolores is a very good cook?'

One of life's basic rules: never praise one woman's cooking to another. 'She's not too bad.'

'Then I'll make certain we have something really nice and I'll do the cooking, not leave it to Margarita. I know I shouldn't say this, but I am a very good cook. Is it terrible to be conceited?'

'Not when there's good cause.'

He arrived home twenty minutes later. He was pouring himself a drink when Dolores came through the bead curtain. 'Well?'

He dropped three ice cubes into the brandy. 'It all worked out.'

'She was obnoxiously rude?'

'On the contrary, quite friendly.'

Her voice sharpened. 'And you, being a man and therefore naive, believed her behaviour to be genuine and not that of someone who smiles when she is angry and praises when she dislikes?'

'You could be forgetting that time changes people.'

'Only for the worse,' she snapped, before she returned into the kitchen.

'Why the hell didn't you say she was real bitchy?' Jaime demanded.

'Because she wasn't,' Alvarez replied.

'But that would have kept Dolores a sight happier.' Jaime drained his glass and refilled it.

Seven

Alvarez read the reports on his desk and these confirmed that, after all the named men had been seen and questioned, only three could be termed suspects: Mercer, Osborn, and Dale. Mercer he'd met, leaving only two to bother him. Gone were the labours of Hercules! Not, of course, that it wasn't going to be too much work.

He looked at his watch. With a little imagination, it was *merienda* time. He made his way downstairs, out on to the narrow street, and through to the old square. Almost every table in front of the cafés was occupied by tourists. When so many had nothing better to do than sit and drink, whilst he had to slave, it was a time of great inequalities.

The bartender in Club Llueso said: 'The usual?'

'Make it a large *coñac*.'

'So what do you think you usually have?'

'A small one.'

'If I ever gave you an ordinary measure, you wouldn't know your tongue was wet. What's got you awkward?'

'Work.'

'Have you suddenly had to do some?'

'I asked for a large *coñac* and a *cortado*, not a chat.'

The bartender muttered something he was careful was not understood, filled one of the containers on the espresso machine and clipped it in place, poured out a brandy, passed the glass across the bar.

Alvarez picked up the glass and studied it. 'Seems you didn't understand.'

'If I handed you the bottle, you'd still moan.'

'Because I don't come in here to pour my own drink.'

'From the look of you, you might lack the strength.'

The bartender moved along to serve another customer. Alvarez, glass in hand, crossed to the only free table by the window. By the time his glass was empty, he decided there was no reason not to be quite cheerful. Questioning Osborn and Dale should not be difficult or time-consuming. Soon, he would be free of the Englishman who had stolen roughly three-quarters of a million euros. How many *coñacs* would that buy?

The bartender brought a cup of coffee to the table.

'Would you like to do something for me?' Alvarez asked.

'No.'

He held up his glass. 'Replace what's evaporated whilst I've had to wait for the coffee.'

As he took the glass, the bartender said, 'Your liver must be more knobbly than the belly of a pregnant sow.'

'Tests have shown it to be in A1 condition.'

'Tests when? Thirty years ago?'

Alvarez stared through the window. A young woman wearing a bikini top and very short skirt went past to become lost in the crowd.

'Put your tongue back in,' the bartender said, as he put a well-filled glass down on the table.

'You can't believe a man will look at a woman and merely admire the grace with which she walks?'

'No.' He left.

Alvarez hesitated to pick up the glass. Was it possible he could be damaging his liver? For fear he might be, should he remember Salom's words? – 'A wise man crossing a field makes certain where he is about to put down his feet.' He would reduce his drinking. Starting tomorrow. He poured some of the brandy into the coffee, drank the rest. Even if it seemed work was not going to be as overwhelming as he had first feared, there would be far too much. There were times when moderation was not really a feasible option. He picked up the glass and carried it to the bar.

He drove to Urbanización Bermejo on Monday morning. The *urbanización* had been built soon after tourism had become a force, but the consequences of it had not been fully appreciated. The bungalows were small, closely packed, and now regarded as downmarket holiday homes; few, if any, were occupied during the winter.

He parked in front of Ca'n Federico, locked the car – with so many foreigners around, one had to be very careful – crossed the pavement, opened the metal gate, which needed painting, and walked up the path that bisected a small area pebbled over except for a circle of earth in which grew a dejected hibiscus, and rang the bell. He could remember when the area had been *garriga* with a few evergreen oaks. Then, it had been useless land, worth a few pesetas the square metre, a suitable heritage for a useless son. Lucky the useless son who had inherited it.

The door was opened by a man who wore short shorts and sandals, whose skin had been newly oiled, and who in no respect matched Faber's description. 'Is Señor Osborn here?' Alvarez asked.

'And if he is?' the other replied aggressively in incorrect, if fluently spoken, Spanish.

Alvarez switched to English. 'I wish to speak to him.'

'Who are you?'

'Inspector Alvarez, Cuerpo General de Policia. And your name is?'

'Smith.'

'And when I look at your passport, will it tell me your

name really is Smith? Or will I have to arrest you for knowingly providing me with false information?'

'Shit! I was only joking.'

'Humour can travel badly. So who are you?'

'Thomas Pollard.'

'Now, is Señor Osborn here, and if he is, will you take me to speak with him?'

Pollard, unable to mask his resentment, led the way into a sitting room with a dining alcove, furnished in the customary tourist style – without taste or quality – through French windows into the rear garden – as at the front, garden in name only.

A man seated on a canvas chair in the sun turned round; his dark glasses concealed his eyes.

'Another sodding detective,' Pollard said, then looked uneasily at Alvarez, belatedly remembering he spoke English.

'What on earth is it now?' Osborn demanded petulantly.

Alvarez said, 'I am sorry to bother you, but I have a few questions I must ask.'

'I told the other policeman we hadn't seen any woman with mauve hair.'

'Orange, señor.'

'It doesn't matter if it's green with mauve spots, we haven't seen her, so you can—'

Pollard interrupted his excited speech. 'Gently, Fred. The police can get rough-handed if they're given cause.'

Osborn stood, picked up a T-shirt and pulled it on. 'It's too hot out here. I'm going inside.'

'I'll stay,' Pollard said.

Alvarez followed Osborn, continuing to assess the other's physical appearance. Assuming his eyes were brown, he could match Faber's description except for his weight, which he thought was probably around 80 kilos. But weight was not as easy to judge as many people believed.

The chairs were more comfortable than appearances suggested and the room was surprisingly cool although it did not have air-conditioning.

'What's the matter this time?' Osborn demanded. 'I've already said we haven't seen this woman.'

'I should like to know if you and Señor Pollard came out on the same flight?'

The question troubled Pollard. 'How does that have anything to do with her?'

'Did you fly out together?'

Osborn moistened his lips. He looked at the French window, as if wishing he could leave quickly. 'I just don't understand why you're asking.'

Alvarez remained silent.

'We didn't,' Osborn finally answered.

'You met here, on the island?'

'Yes.'

'Where?'

'At . . . at a bar.'

Alvarez had the experience to imagine the circumstances with a good degree of accuracy. Pollard's Spanish suggested a considerable time in Spain, learning the language haphazardly; his appearance and manner were those of a beachcomber who frequented bars where there were likely to be many English, in search of someone who would payroll him. Always short of money, if there were an opportunity to steal, he would, knowing the victim would be reluctant to report the theft. It was possible he had already been the subject of a police investigation and that would explain the contradiction of his aggressiveness yet acknowledgement of the stupidity of antagonizing the police. It might be worth contacting other areas to find if theft in such circumstances had been reported. As far as the search for Faber was concerned, Pollard was of no consequence. 'Where do you live in England?'

'Why d'you want to know?'

Alvarez did not answer. The more nervous and flustered Osborn became, the more threatening silence might become.

'Look, I'm just here on holiday.'

'I understand that, but I still need to know.'

'You're not thinking of . . .'

'Thinking of what?'

There was no answer.

'What is your address in England?'

Osborn spoke with a rush of words. 'A hundred and five, Montague Drive, Hanwell.'

'What kind of work do you do, señor?'

'I'm a statistician.'

A job which demanded a smart brain – an even smarter one if called upon to interpret the statistics. So Osborn had a sharp mind, but a weak character. He could probably plan a complex fraud with no trouble, but would he have the courage to carry it out? 'Would you please remove your dark glasses?'

'Why? . . . What's going on?'

'If you would take them off.'

Osborn's eyes were, as reported, dark brown. 'That is all. Thank you for your help, señor.' Alvarez left, certain Osborn had become a very worried man.

Dolores stepped through the bead curtain into the sitting/dining room. 'You will both make certain you are here on time for supper this evening.'

'Because you're cooking something delicious?' Alvarez asked.

'You believe that only happens occasionally?'

'Every time you cook. What I meant was, it will be notable even when measured against your standards of perfection.'

'When a woman praises, it is to please; when a man praises, it is either because he wants something or to hide something.'

'Perhaps tuna with salsa de Romesco?'

She did not answer.

'*Lubina con pinoñes y pasas*?'

'You will have to wait and see.' She returned into the kitchen.

Alvarez lifted up the bottle of Soberano to find it was empty. He leaned over, opened the Mallorquin sideboard with carved doors, and brought out an unopened bottle. He stripped off the excise label, unscrewed the cap, refilled his glass, passed the bottle to Jaime.

Dolores reappeared. She folded her arms across her chest and regarded them sharply. 'This evening, I shall be slaving for hours in the furnace-hot kitchen because I believe it is a wife's duty to please her husband and cousin, even though their expressed appreciation of my effort is as likely as meeting a politician who is honest. So for once you will make certain that before supper you do not drink until a fog descends across your minds.' She unfolded her arms and returned into the kitchen.

Jaime heard sounds that suggested Dolores was busy. 'Drinking's never stopped me enjoying a good meal. And it improves a bad meal.' He hurriedly added, in case his words had been heard in the kitchen, 'Not that one ever has one of those here.'

Alvarez studied his glass. Earlier, he had promised self-denial to ensure future health, simply because of what the bartender had said. Absurd! Even if there were a grain of truth in what had been suggested, life taught the wise that the future could never be planned. Deny oneself cigarettes and alcohol to ensure an old age and fate would arrange for one to be run over by a car. He dropped four cubes of ice from the insulated container into his glass and covered them with brandy.

'What's with women that they go on and on about us men drinking?' Jaime asked in a low voice.

It had not been low enough. 'You would like to know?' Dolores demanded, as she swept back through the bead curtain. 'It is because, when they drink to excess, they speak absurdities, find humour in situations which are fit only to be experienced by women who have lost all self-respect.'

'That's all balls!'

'Clearly, you have already drunk far too freely.'

He indicated his empty glass. 'That is my first.'

'Your first after the last.'

'What's that supposed to bloody mean?'

'Your speech is about to become unfit for a decent woman to listen to.' She withdrew into the kitchen.

'I'll bet she tells all her women friends that I am a dipsomaniac,' Jaime said.

'I would wish to publish my private shame?' she called out.

'Ears like radar,' he mumbled.

Alvarez pushed the bottle across the table. Jaime looked at it, at his empty glass, at the bead curtain; as he reached out to grip the neck of the bottle, a swirl of air caused several of the strings of beads to clash together and he jerked his hand away as if the glass had become red-hot.

The scent of a million euros wouldn't turn him into a tiger, Alvarez thought scornfully.

They were drinking coffee when Dolores said, 'I wonder what Raquel eats?'

'Food,' Jaime said.

'You think that amusing?'

'When someone asks a question . . .'

'The meaning of which is understood by those whose minds are not befogged.'

'But the way you spoke . . .'

'Was perfectly intelligible.' She picked up one of the petit fours she had bought that morning. 'Is that not so?' she asked Alvarez before she put the small biscuit into her mouth.

He carefully did not answer.

She swallowed. 'It is an illogical world in which I live. When my husband drinks, he becomes childishly loquacious; when my cousin drinks, he becomes dumb.'

He was dumb because her mention of Raquel had caused him to remember. How could he ever have forgotten? Was his failing memory the result of a failing liver?

'Perhaps you find my conversation boring?'

He hurried to answer: 'Far from it. It is always a pleasure to speak with you.'

'Then why do you ignore what I say?'

Why did life delight in conflict? Why did Dolores decide to prepare a special meal on the same evening as he had arranged to have dinner with Raquel?

Dolores drank the last of the coffee in her cup, turned to Jaime. 'Perhaps you are still conscious. What do you imagine Raquel eats off?'

'Plates?'

'As my dear mother used to say, "If a woman could glimpse the future, she would never marry" . . . Raquel will have the finest porcelain money can buy in order to impress her guests. But perhaps that is not so. Since she lacks all restraint, it is probable she feasts off gold.' She pushed her chair back and stood. 'Since to ask either of you to help me clear the table would be to suggest I do not learn from experience, I will not ask. Do not disturb yourselves.' She collected up plates and cutlery, carried some through to the kitchen.

'Does anyone really eat off gold?' Jaime asked.

'What's that?' Alvarez said.

'She's right about you!'

How the hell, Alvarez wondered, could he tell Dolores he would not be at home that evening for the special meal and not arouse her fury?

She returned with the garishly patterned tray which Isabel had bought her at the local Christmas market and was a prized possession. She loaded the tray, picked it up.

Alvarez coughed. 'I . . . I am afraid I am not here.'

'So where has the drink taken you?'

'I mean, I can't be here for supper. I'll have to be working. Salas has told me to find and question two men whose evidence is very important in a case that's starting in Palma tomorrow.'

'You cannot search for them this afternoon?'

'They won't be arriving in the Port before eight.'

'Then why are they not questioned where they are now?'

'It's not known where they are.'

'Then how can it be certain they will arrive after eight?'

'Word has come through.'

She replaced the tray on the table with sufficient force to make things on it rattle. 'Aiyee! But you must think me simple to expect me to believe you.'

'How can you imagine I would miss one of your special meals unless I had no option?'

'By allowing your imagination to feed you.'

'What imagination?'

'That which tells an old man, when he looks in a mirror, he sees a young, handsome Lothario.'

'I am not an old man.'

'To a young woman, you are the past.'

'I have to carry out Salas's orders.'

'You worry more about your duty than your belly? Has the moon stopped turning around the earth? I will tell you why you scorn the food I serve after slaving for so many hours. You are meeting a woman. Young, because you yearn for your lost youth; attractive since you are only interested in the wrapping; foreign because she will have no morals.'

'I am not meeting a young, foreign woman.'

'She is not so young? You have finally had to learn that an aging cockerel cannot run as fast as a young pullet?'

Her unflattering comments caused him to say bitterly, 'Who has been telling me for years that at my age – which is not great – I should be –' He stopped abruptly. Reminding her that she had repeatedly advised him to meet a Mallorquin woman of his own age with possessions was not a tactful thing to say when it must become obvious he was referring to Raquel and intended to enjoy her food rather than Dolores's.

'You should be . . . what?'

'I've forgotten.'

'With your brain swimming in alcohol, I am surprised you can even think of something to forget.' She picked up the tray and carried it through to the kitchen.

Eight

Both life and a siesta were basically tragic since each had to end. Alvarez reluctantly dressed and made his way downstairs to the kitchen. Dolores had made some coffee, but it became clear her mood was not as forgiving as that might suggest. She did not pour it out for him; and when he asked for some *coca*, she replied there was only a small piece, left from yesterday, because she had been too tired to go out and shop. If he wanted that, it was in the cupboard.

He sat at the table and drank two cups of coffee, ate the stale *coca*, and sadly reflected that these days women no longer possessed a sense of duty.

He left the house, climbed into his car, drove along the narrow roads designed for mule carts and across the *torrente*, now with dry bedrock, occasionally a raging and dangerous flood. At the Laraix road he was forced to wait for a gaggle of cyclists and he stared at the mountains, a kilometre to the north. Irregular in shape, some clothed in pine trees, others bare of vegetation, they possessed an ever-varying character. In sunny weather, they were benign; under dark cloud and rain, they gloomed.

A car hooted. In his rear-view mirror, he recognized the long bonnet of a black Mercedes. The horn sounded again. A German driver, demanding a passage of might? A Frenchman, contemptuous of Spanish lethargy? An Englishman, pressing the button by mistake? . . . He turned right, continued along to the roundabout designed by a humorist, drove towards the *urbanización* hugging the side of the mountain and turned off just short of it.

Ca'n Trestar was the last of six buildings on land that had once been a worthless tangle of wild olive, evergreen oak, pine trees, prickly pear cacti, and brambles; the cost of clearing it could never have been regained by farming since the soil was of poor quality and rocky. Foreigners had bought it, cleared it and built on it at great profit to the Mallorquins, confirming to them that more than one was born every day.

The bungalow was of modest size and lacked any hint of architectural inspiration; it was backed by a wavy line of wild olive trees and surrounded by a small garden in which plants grew if well watered and fertilized and then only with great difficulty.

Alvarez climbed out of the Ibiza. Despite all the years he had lived and worked in Llueso, he had not once been along this road – a strange fact and one that might, might it not, hold some special significance for him. He opened the wooden gate, set in a low stone wall, walked up to the front door and rang the bell. Here the mountain was very close and formed a jagged wall of steep rocks; they were not benign even in sharp sunshine.

The door was opened by a man dressed in swimming trunks; his brown hair and costume showed signs of dampness, his body appeared dry.

'Señor Dale?' Alvarez asked.

'Yes?'

'I am Inspector Alvarez, Cuerpo General de Policia. I should like to have a word with you.'

'You'd better come in.'

Dale's appearance, apart from the receding hairline, lay within the parameters of the written description of Faber. Yet so had Osborn's and Mercer's, and none of the three resembled either of the other two. Which showed how inexact an image a written description could evoke in persons' minds. A point to make to Salas when it became necessary to explain why little progress was being made.

He followed Dale through to a small sitting room – again furnished for tourists – and out to a narrow patio with an overhead awning, which had been clumsily repaired following a long tear. Beyond the patio was a small pool in which a man was swimming. Dale said, 'My friend, George Varley.'

Varley stopped swimming and stood; the water reached to his waist. 'Who's honouring us with a visit?' he asked lightly.

'Inspector Alvarez.'

'Another copper! What makes us so interesting? Has a local bank been robbed? If so, we can assure the inspector we are innocent, since we're on holiday.'

'One day, George,' Dale said sourly, 'your so-called sense of humour is going to cause trouble.'

'I shall plead lack of intent since it was unconscious humour.' He ploughed through the water to the steps, climbed them.

Varley was handsome, broad-shouldered, his body slim and muscular. He came to a halt a couple of metres from Alvarez. 'Inspector, I don't think you have yet been offered a drink. A serious breach of local manners.'

Alvarez agreed but was annoyed by the hint of sarcasm which might infer the Mallorquins drank copiously.

'I hasten to ask what you would like? I am assuming that you are not, as in puritanical England, precluded from drinking when on duty.'

'It is left to our discretion.'

'Would I be correct to think of you as a man with a practical discretion?'

You, Alvarez thought, are one smart-arse. 'May I have a *coñac* with just ice?'

'In the basket of goodies which met us on arrival was a bottle of brandy and since neither Terry nor I drink it, that is no problem.'

Welcome baskets seldom contained *coñac* of which one could approve.

'Do sit, Inspector, while I fetch the drinks.' Varley went into the bungalow.

Alvarez sat on one of the patio chairs within the shade of the awning, Dale beside him.

After a long pause, Dale said, 'It's very hot.'

'Indeed, señor.'

'Is it always this hot?'

'Quite often, but the weather can be very variable in May.'

'Because it is an island?'

'I imagine so.' Hardly an invigorating conversation, Alvarez thought; more like one between two persons, one of whom would have preferred to be on his own.

Varley wheeled out a trolley on which were bottles, glasses, and an ice bucket. 'Inspector, if I remember correctly, you said just ice with the brandy. Terry, the usual?'

'Yes.'

'Drinks will be served as soon as possible.'

As Varley picked up a bottle, unscrewed the cap and began to pour, Dale said, 'Do you have much work, Inspector?'

'Far too much, señor,' Alvarez replied.

'I wouldn't have thought there was all that much crime here.'

'There isn't where only Mallorquins are concerned.' Alvarez never hesitated to defend local honour. 'Unfortunately, the foreigners can create a great deal of trouble.'

'I suppose . . .' Dale stopped when he saw Varley's approaching.

Varley put glasses down on the table, sat, raised his. 'To health, wealth, and happiness.'

Alvarez was relieved to discover the brandy was of slightly better quality than he had expected.

'Have we heard the reason for your visit?' Varley asked.

'I need to ask some questions.'

'About the missing woman?'

'That is so.'

'Then I fear you visit will be a failure. We told the other chap all we could and it amounted to nothing. Which was sad, because there are times when one wishes to help the police, not hinder them.'

'Stop it,' Dale said sharply.

'Stop exactly what?'

'Talking stupidly and giving the wrong impression.'

'I'm sure the inspector understands that while normally we civilians are happier if authority is held at arm's length, there can be times when we open our arms wide. Did we know anything of the slightest relevance, we would rush to report it.'

'Since speaking to my colleague, señor, you have not seen a woman in a restaurant, bar, in the streets, sunbathing or swimming, who might be the one we seek?'

'I fear not.'

Alvarez drank. He replaced the glass on the table. 'Did you and Señor Varley fly here together?'

Dale said, 'How we came here can't be of any interest to you.'

'The less his apparent interest,' Varley said, 'the more his actual interest.'

'Can't you stop talking nonsense?'

'There has to be truth for there to be nonsense.' He

turned to Alvarez. 'Suppose I suggest you have no interest in a missing woman with strangely coloured hair?'

'You are entitled to your own opinion.'

'Would it be wrong to find significance in the apparent irrelevance of some of your questions?'

'I do not waste my time asking irrelevant questions.'

'Quite. So one assumes the irrelevance is only apparent.'

In the old days, an obnoxious foreigner could be thrown off the island for irrelevant reasons.

'Perhaps you are pursuing an investigation which has to be hidden from the public?'

Thrown off after a suitable time in a small and smelly cell. 'Señor, you did not fly here with Señor Dale.'

'First the query, then the answer.'

'When did you arrive?'

'I suspect we are approaching relevance.'

'You are unwilling to answer?'

'Let me ask you a question: are you agreed we are no longer in search of a young lady with frizzy ginger hair?'

Varley, Alvarez judged, had the nerve, the self-confidence and the insolent contempt of authority to have carried out the theft. However, by no stretch of the imagination could he be Faber. Yet nothing in the report from England determined only one man had been concerned; could not one have planned, another executed? Varley's manner, ironic and challenging because of a belief in his own cleverness, might be betraying him. If Dale was Faber . . .

'The silence suggests you have much to consider, Inspector,' Varley said.

'I am waiting for you to say when you arrived here?'

'Without explaining why you ask.'

Alvarez drank.

'I stepped on to these shores at the beginning of April.'

'Why did you come here?'

'After it had been raining, seemingly without a break,

for months, I decided that if I didn't very soon enjoy sunshine, I'd collapse into a Stygian gloom.'

'You were not working?'

'Yes, I was. But these days, switching jobs demonstrates initiative and ambition. When I decide to return to England, I will seek fresh employment and if I don't find it within a couple of weeks, I shall be very surprised.'

'When did you meet Señor Dale?'

'Not very long ago.'

'Where?'

'At an ice-cream stall down by the harbour. We both chose pistachio, which clearly demonstrated a mutual interest.'

Alvarez spoke to Dale. 'Señor, when did you arrive here?'

'Why do you want to know?'

'The hidden agenda,' Varley said.

'It will save everyone much time and trouble if you tell me now, señor.'

'The twenty-first.'

'Of this month?'

'Yes.'

'You are married?'

'No.'

'Where do you live?'

'Why are you asking all these questions?'

'Because I wish to know the answers.'

'Why?'

Alvarez did not answer. After a while, Dale muttered, 'Arlington Cross.'

'Where is that?'

'Kent.'

'Is it near Eddington?'

'No.'

'What is your work?'

'Security.'

'In which branch?'

'I make certain the firm's lines and records remain uncorrupted.'

'You work with computers?'

'Yes.'

'What is the firm's name?'

'Hillsdale and Co.'

On Dale's forehead, the hair had receded to leave a V. It was a physical feature he would have expected to be noted, but then he was a trained observer. And if Dale combed his hair further to one side, the V would be far less noticeable. 'Thank you, señor, for your help.'

'Does that mean no more questions?'

'Never encourage authority,' Varley said, and laughed.

Alvarez left. The brandy had proved less crude than it could have been, so they might have offered him a second glass.

The phone rang. Alvarez reached across his desk and lifted the receiver.

'The superior chief will speak to you.'

The worst possible start to an evening. Why was Salas still at work and not at home, irritating his family?

'What do you have to report?' Salas asked.

'With regard to the Faber case, señor? I have already questioned several men.'

'Surprising!'

'Why is that?'

'If it is not obvious, it would be a waste of time to explain.'

'There is the possibility I have identified Faber. Broadly speaking, Terry Dale matches his description, with one exception, negative rather than positive. Of course, negative can be as good a positive as a positive in certain circumstances . . .'

'Which can be ignored.'

'He lives in Kent, somewhere called Arlington Cross. When I asked him if that was near Eddington, he said not. Which is interesting, because I checked how far apart the two towns are on a map of England which my niece – niece by sentiment rather than blood – had from school—'

'I am uninterested in your domestic arrangements.'

'According to this map, the two towns are no more than six miles apart. I think that is about ten kilometres. Most people would call that fairly close.'

'Well?'

'You remember Eddington is where Faber lived?'

'You are trying to be insulting?'

'Certainly not.'

'Then why infer I am unaware of an important fact?'

'It's just you didn't seem immediately to grasp the possible significance . . .'

'Whether or not it is your intention to be insolent, you are succeeding. No doubt, you failed to determine whether Dale has any knowledge of computing.'

'He has a considerable knowledge. In addition, clearly my questions disturbed him.'

'Confused is more likely. Have you called him to the post to question him officially?'

'Not yet.'

'Why not?'

'There are problems. He suffers from noticeable hair recession at the forehead. There is no mention of this in the written description.'

'You should not assume the English can produce a competent report.'

'Then there is Varley . . .'

'Who?'

'George Varley. That he is Dale's current partner is clear from the way in which—'

'You will not pursue the matter.'

'If Varley is lying – and I am sure he finds it easier to lie than tell the truth – he might well have played an important part. Faber may have given him the security information to enter the files of Finch and Abbott . . .'

'Who?'

'You do not remember . . .'

'What the devil are you now trying to suggest I have forgotten?'

'That was the firm for whom Faber worked in England.'

'I am perfectly well aware of that. It should have been obvious to someone of even mean intelligence that I was reminding you that in order to deliver a competent report, every name mentioned needs to be identified.'

'But if you know whom I'm talking about—'

'It appears to be a complete waste of time trying to make you understand the demands of an efficient officer. Continue with your report.'

'One needs to consider the possibility that, with the facts Dale might have provided, Varley carried out the actual fraud here, on the island. Computer fraud, unlike other kinds, can be carried out at a distance. A man here can just as easily hack into the secrets of a firm in England as someone who is there. Dale claims he worked for Hillsdale and Company, in the security section; Finch and Abbott, the firm which was swindled—'

'Is it really necessary to repeat yourself a dozen times?'

'You said I should identify every name I mention, señor.'

'There are times, Alvarez, when I am convinced that were you to enter an IQ test, you would be the first recorded negative value.'

'Of course, the coincidences – Dale's resembling Faber's description, living near Eddington, working in computers, arriving here soon after the theft, friendship with Varley – could be just coincidences, but the more coincidences there are, the less coincidental they can become . . .'

'Do you, or do you not, believe Dale to be Faber?'

'Yes and no, señor.'

'Were there a third possibility, you would no doubt advance that as well.'

'He showed nervousness and also resentment at my questioning. As a man, he is unimpressive, so he might have the ability to conceive and plan the fraud but lack the nerve to carry it out. Yet even so, he does not seem to have that edge which allows a man knowingly to break the law.'

'And you lack the ability to fasten on an important point. He lied about not living near Eddington. An innocent man does not needlessly lie.'

'One has to remember that his scales may be different. What I consider close, he may not. We aren't all mentally similar.'

'For which one has to be grateful. Clearly, he was trying to mislead you, understanding the importance of the question far better than you. You can inform the English police that in investigating the impossible task they—'

'Señor.'

'Must you interrupt me?'

'Very soon after we received the request to identify Faber, I said it was an impossible task. You told me the Cuerpo does not recognize the word "impossible".'

'I remember no such incident. You will inform the English authorities—'

'Señor, I don't think it is yet time to be at all positive.'

'On this island, it is never the time to do anything. You will photograph Dale, write a report – you had better submit that to me so that I can expunge all illiteracies – and send both to England.'

'In the circumstances, wouldn't it be best to express doubt

by asking if the photo does identify Faber, rather than admitting we think it does? Then if we are wrong—'

'An efficient officer does not consider failure.'

'But there have to be times when it's best to play safe. I remember last year, when the director-general was querying that report of yours, you told me to—'

'You will do as I say without any further argument.' Salas rang off.

Salas had given the order, so he was responsible for the consequences; but life seldom worked like that. Far from accepting that one should reap what one had sown, seniors made a habit of blaming their stupidity and incompetence on their juniors.

Alvarez reached down, opened the bottom right-hand drawer of the desk, brought out bottle and glass, poured himself a solid brandy. He emptied the glass and was about to refill it when he accepted he should forego a second drink if he was going to arrive at Sa Echona only slightly late.

Nine

Raquel had left the smaller sitting room to make certain her cooking was progressing well and Alvarez stared out of the wide window to the left. Old Eduardo had been a man of the earth who had delighted in boasting about the olives, almonds, oranges, lemons, grapefruit, mandarins, persimmons, apples, pears, plums and loquats his trees grew – the finest, most prolific trees on the island. His land had been in such good heart that the tomatoes, peppers, lemons, onions, garlic, beans, peas, cauliflowers, cabbages, melons and strawberries it produced had been unsurpassed anywhere.

She returned and sat. 'We'll eat in twenty minutes, if that's all right with you?'

'Of course.' It was a pleasant change to be in the company of a woman who consulted rather than ordered.

'I've decided to give you a dish I do rather well . . . I shouldn't say that, but you already know I'm absolutely shameless about my own cooking.'

'With reason, I'm quite certain.'

'A rash thing to say before you've eaten!'

'What are you cooking?'

'*Lechazos de dos madres*. I hope you like it.'

'I most certainly will.' It was a dish Dolores had never served because the ingredients were so expensive and normally unobtainable: a lamb suckled by two ewes and not allowed to feed on grass, in order to produce a superb quality flesh. Some termed it the caviar of meat.

'And we're starting with grilled prawns. I managed to find some large ones – they're so much more succulent . . . I imagine you enjoy your food?'

'I suppose I do.'

'And Dolores makes certain you feed well?'

That was the second time she had asked him; again, he answered with as much discretion as possible. 'She is quite a cook.'

'She always was good at everything. Are you?'

'Not really.'

'You're just being modest! I'll bet you are a first-class detective.'

'The superior chief would disagree with that.'

'Then he's stupid.' Her trust was gratifying. 'Do you like your work?'

'It's not too bad.'

'But you're not overenthusiastic about it?'

'I'd much rather be independent, not always having someone telling me what to do and criticizing me when I do it.'

'What would you prefer to do?'

Nothing, was one answer; 'I've always wanted to farm' was another.

'Then why haven't you?'

'My father sold his land to a speculator because he did not understand what it would become worth. He used the money to give my mother the small luxuries she had never known before. So I haven't been able to buy a finca.'

'These days, there can't be many Mallorquins with an ambition to farm.'

'There aren't. It's much easier to earn many times more in the tourist trade.'

'But you wouldn't want to do that?'

'I'd rather suffer my present job.'

She laughed. 'A damning opinion of tourists! What would you farm?'

'First of all, the traditional crops, but I'd import fresh seed, not harvest my own as so many still do, because that leads to deterioration. I'd always go for quality, not quantity. When I was young, a tomato was filled with taste; now it has none, because it is picked green and has to ripen off the plant in order to travel further and better. Perhaps the young of today will never know how a ripe tomato should taste.'

'You sound like a farming evangelist!'

'Then I must apologize.'

'Don't be silly. It's wonderful hearing such enthusiasm. Would that Rafael were the same.'

'Rafael?'

'My manager. He worked for Uncle Eduardo when Uncle's health was fading and he wasn't able to demand a day's work for a day's wage. I ask Rafael to do something and he finds a dozen reasons for not doing it. His generation don't believe in taking any notice of what a woman says and he's become slack. If there were a man to give orders – you, for instance – and see them carried out, I imagine he'd probably become a good worker again, though never one ready to experiment.'

The words had been very casually spoken. Had the thought behind them been equally so? Was she thinking that he had the capability to restore the full fruitfulness the estate had once known?

'Your glass is empty, Enrique.'

He was surprised to note that this was so.

'I must make a final check that everything is all right, so will you pour yourself another drink?' She left the room, moving with grace.

The sideboard was made from a wood with a tight grain and a deep red colour which glowed from constant polishing; the lion handles were bright. The cognac was Hennessey XO. Here, he thought as he poured, a man would live like a king.

He returned to his seat, sipped the cognac to which he had added only one cube of ice – he did not want to appear to be the peasant he was. If Rafael had become so slack, there would be a great deal of work necessary. Trees, especially the oranges, would need pruning and treating for fungal infections; the earth would have to be fed, irrigation restored. Self-sufficiency had ceased to be realistically practicable, so many decisions would have to be made. Should the vines once used for wine be grubbed up, since the probability was they were an old variety and, no matter how much care was given to them, incapable of producing a good wine? Would one bother to replace them when Marqués de Riscal and Imperial were readily available to someone with the money to buy them?

'Where are you, Enrique?'

He started, not having heard her return.

'A thousand kilometres away?'

'I was thinking what life would be like if I were a farmer.'

'You would not have come here when I stupidly reported my jewellery had been stolen.' She had spoken as if she would have regretted his non-appearance.

They stood in the hall in which were several pieces of antique Mallorquin furniture, practical, yet clumsy when compared with those in the rooms.

'I'm so glad you liked the meal,' she said.

'It was superb.'

'Nearly as good as Dolores feeds you?'

'Better,' he answered rashly, awash with Vega Sicilia and Hennessey XO.

'Praise indeed! It has been fun cooking for someone

who really appreciates what he eats. I wonder . . . Would you like to come again?'

He was surprised she needed to ask.

'It can be rather boring on my own and there's little point in cooking something special just to please myself. Added to which, Margarita would be much happier eating the simple food she had when she was young . . . You'd be doing me a favour.'

'Not nearly as great a one as you'd be giving me,' he said, proud of his gallantry.

'What could be more satisfying than for each of us to favour the other? When shall we say?'

'I can't be certain what I'm doing next week . . .'

'You would like to wait that long?'

'I didn't want to seem . . . well, too eager.'

'What a charming thing to say! Today is Monday. So let's name Thursday, unless you tell me you have to spend the evening peering through a magnifying glass at some unmentionable horror.'

'I don't think I've ever used a magnifying glass.'

'You're beginning to destroy an image! . . . Thursday it is, then. I won't ask you what you'd like because I have a juvenile delight in surprising someone. Just tell me what you don't like.'

'I can't think of anything.'

'It seems we have a lot in common.'

He said goodnight and left. On the drive home he enjoyed the fantasy of whether they might soon have even more in common.

Dolores and Jaime were watching television.

Jaime looked up. 'You're back early.'

'It's nearly half eleven.'

'But seeing you were in luck, I didn't expect you until the sun was up.'

'My husband,' Dolores said to no one in particular, 'considers good luck to be the opportunity to betray one's wife, family, and honour.'

'I've not done anything and Enrique's not married.'

'It is the principle.'

'What principle?'

She ignored him, spoke to Alvarez. 'You were successful?'

'You've only got to look at him to know he was,' Jaime said. 'The dog found its way into the butcher's shop.'

Alvarez spoke sourly. 'I have not spent the evening as everyone is determined to believe.'

'Then you met them?' she asked.

'Met who?'

'How right my mother was when she said that when a man cannot remember, it is because guilt blocks his memory. I decide to prepare a special meal – even though it means I will have to slave all day and my sacrifice will not be appreciated since a man is concerned only with himself. I tell my cousin what I intend to do and he says he cannot be present because he has to meet two men whose evidence is so very important.'

Alvarez hastened to remedy his gaffe. 'It was essential because—'

'Do not strain your imagination.'

'I met them in the port and they were able to give me the information I needed.'

She stood. 'Women enjoy but one favour from life. They can judge when a man is lying.' She crossed to the stairs, began to climb them, stopped, spoke to Jaime. 'You are not coming to bed?'

'I thought I'd watch the rest of the programme.'

'Or the film on one of the other channels which would be immediately turned off if I remained here?' She resumed climbing the stairs.

Jaime waited until she was out of sight and said, 'D'you think she's right?'

'Look and see if there's something ripe on.'

'I mean, is she right that women can tell if a man's lying?'

'They're always so suspicious, that's immaterial.'

Jaime thought for a moment, then said, 'She picked you out right enough. She knew your story of meeting men down in the port was ridiculous, that you were missing out on her meal because you'd something sweeter on your plate. Come on, lighten up and tell me what the latest is like.'

'Even more voracious than her sister.'

'Two of 'em . . . Why are you such a lucky bastard?'

'Because I lead a sober, industrious, virtuous life.'

Ten

Alvarez braked to a halt, switched off the engine, climbed out of the Ibiza and walked the few metres to the front door of Villa Bellavista. He rang the bell, turned and stared at the garden. Keeping it in order, along with other gardens around villas let to tourists, was a prime example of the modern tendency to waste time and effort. Nothing edible was grown.

The door opened. 'If you want . . .' Susan began in poor Spanish. Then in English: 'It's you.'

'Good morning, señora.'

'I suppose you want Steve. I'm sorry, but I think he's away for the day.'

'Then I'll have a word with you and your husband.'

'What about?'

'It is still possible you may be able to help me.'

'But—'

'May I come in?'

He followed her into the sitting room. Her skirt was surprisingly short. She had graceful legs.

'You want to speak to Dick and me? Dick's working at a couple of other properties.'

'Are they near here?'

'One is. The family have three kids who've dragged up many of the plants and he's hopefully replacing them. Perhaps also explaining to the parents that a package holiday does not include the right of destruction.'

'Do you think he could return for a moment a little later?'

'If the kids haven't trapped him in a pit lined with pointed bamboos. In any case, he may turn up for some coffee. Saying which, would you like some now?'

'Thank you, I should.'

'And I remember you enjoy a brandy with it?'

'That is true.'

'I'm sure Steve would offer you one, so I'll set things up. Or would you rather talk first?'

'I prefer to observe the priorities.'

It was a couple of seconds before she smiled, suggesting his answer had momentarily confused her. She left.

A woman didn't have to be very beautiful to attract a man's interest, so what exactly was it that did? A perfect body? Perfection could become boring. An arch manner? Archness often meant self-approval. A hint of wantonness? Perhaps, but no more than a hint or there would be no chase and uncertainty was necessary for complete pleasure. He couldn't decide if Susan's manner was touched with wantonness or merely a lack of self. She was very friendly. Previously, when serving coffee, she had leaned over further than advisable in a dress with generous décolletage and when not wearing a brassière, but she might as easily have been aware as unaware of that. It was also possible she had presumed him to be too much of a gentleman to look.

She returned, crossed to where he sat, set a small tray on the occasional table. 'Do help yourself to milk and sugar.'

He was sorry she did not offer to pour the milk. Perhaps she was remembering; perhaps she had decided he was not a gentleman. 'Aren't you having coffee?'

'I had a cup just before you arrived . . . Does your being here again mean you still haven't found the missing woman?'

'I'm afraid so.'

'We're not going to be able to help. Is her relative still alive?'

'As far as we know.'

'Let's hope she recovers.'

'Indeed, because hope is all that's left . . . Do you enjoy your work, señora?'

'When people aren't too objectionable.'

'There are many who are?'

'Some try to treat me as a skivvy.'

'I should be surprised if Señor Mercer ever behaves like that.'

'He doesn't. And he keeps his hands to himself.'

'That is not always the case?'

'Are you a hundred years out of date? Last week one of the men tried to paw me every time his wife wasn't in the same room. In the end Dick had to get hold of him and tell him to behave.'

'I understand Señor Mercer is not married?'

'Hardly surprising.'

'Why do you say that?'

'You haven't guessed?'

'Guessed?'

'When he entertains, he entertains men.'

'He told me he hopes to become a writer.'

'It'll be a long time before that happens unless he sits down and tries.'

'Perhaps he is looking for inspiration. I understand that is what writers say when they are doing nothing. It must be quite a change, being here instead of in an office, dealing with agricultural machinery.'

'With what?'

'Tractors, combines . . .'

'I do know what agricultural machinery means.'

'I am sorry.'

'It's just . . . There's Dick.'

Through the window he saw Thorne approach the front door. 'Your husband looks as if his leg is hurting him a lot today.'

'It is worse some days. Still, the surgeon did a wonderful job on his leg, if not his brain.'

'He was injured in the head as well?'

'Sorry, I'm confusing everyone. After the accident, and for a time after the operation, there were so many things he couldn't do, he became totally frustrated. That's what brought us here. I decided we had to make a clean break in life or our marriage could become rocky. It was a gamble, a jump into the dark; but, thank God, it's worked. I got a job with the letting agency; to begin with he couldn't find anyone who wanted him and the frustration started to build up again. Then one of the gardeners quit and I asked the boss to take him on. At first he wouldn't, said he wasn't up to doing the job; I told him he was and would prove it by working for nothing for a fortnight. No employer can refuse that kind of offer. His lack of Spanish isn't really a hindrance because mostly the clients are English and the boss boasts he speaks the language like a native.'

Thorne came into the room. Alvarez greeted him. Thorne looked enquiringly at his wife.

'They still haven't found the girl,' she said, 'and the inspector wondered if we'd seen anything fresh.'

He gripped the arm of a chair to ease himself into a sitting position.

'Is it bad today?' she asked.

'I gave it a bit of a twist when I was replanting one of the roses the kids had torn up.'

'I'll get you some paracetamol.'

'There's no need.'

'Don't be ridiculous.' She stood.

'Is there any more coffee?'

'Enough for one cup.' She crossed to the door, came to a halt. 'What kind of work did Steve tell us he'd been doing back home?'

'Finance. Dealt in millions that were just figures on a screen and disappeared at the press of a button. I often remember his saying that money became so illusory he had to remind himself that what he actually spent was real and had to be earned.'

'I knew I wasn't wrong. The inspector thought he worked in agricultural machinery.'

'Steve wouldn't know the difference between barley and oats.'

She went through the doorway and out of sight.

'It sounds as if Señor Mercer must have a sharp brain,' Alvarez commented. 'I suppose he writes his book on a computer?'

'A laptop. Inordinately proud of it and has told me time and again that it's umpteen times more powerful than the computer they used to land on the moon.'

Susan returned with a mug of coffee in one hand, two pills in the other. 'I'm not moving until I see you swallow them.'

'Suspicion personified!'

She spoke to Alvarez. 'Why are men so reluctant to take medicine?'

'I don't know, señora.'

'I suppose they think it upsets their manly image.'

Thorne put the pills in his mouth and drank.

When he left, some twenty-five minutes later, Susan apologized for their not being able to help. It was clear she had no idea that, on the contrary, she and her husband had perhaps helped him considerably.

Eleven

Alvarez slumped down in his chair behind the desk. Life was in one of its grimmer phases. Lunch, by Dolores's standards, had been poor – hers was not a forgiving nature; the afternoon was very hot for May; he had had to park well away from the post so that the walk had left him sweating and short of breath; the duty *cabo* had insolently remarked that he looked like a man overdue his pension . . . His eyelids closed and the grim world slipped away.

The phone awoke him. More trouble, he pessimistically judged. He was correct. Salas's secretary said, in her plum-laden voice, that the superior chief wished to speak to him.

'Where is your report?' was Salas's greeting.

'Señor, I have been pursuing investigations . . .'

'From an armchair? I wish to inform London we have identified Faber, but if I do so, they will ask for the papers to be faxed to them. I would have to reply that they would be sent by post. Do you know why?'

'No, señor.'

'Post would explain the delay in receipt. Why should I welcome this delay? Because I have no doubt that you have not yet written any report or obtained a photograph of Dale. Is that correct?'

'There has been so much to do . . .'

'Little of which will have been done. On this island, "now" is a rarely used word, "tomorrow" one denoting unusual haste.'

'Señor, I think it is as well that no report has been sent.'

'You rejoice in inefficiency?'

'I don't think Dale is Faber.'

'Do you know what you are saying?'

'Dale did initially appear a possible suspect, but having spoken to the Thornes, who are the couple who look after the bungalow Steven Mercer rents through Morgan and Gaya – they are the letting agents who handle Villa Bellavista . . .'

'Are they left-handed?'

'Señor?'

'Do you think I have nothing better to do than listen to a mass of irrelevant information?'

'You told me I must always identify names.'

'I am beginning to believe that you employ verbal stupidity as a means of dumb insolence.'

'But if I speak, I'm not dumb . . .'

'Silence!'

After a moment, Salas said, 'You have nothing to add other than the fact that you have changed your mind on a whim?'

'Not a whim, señor. What I have learned from the Thornes contradicts what Mercer told me and makes it clear he worked in a financial firm, is very conversant with computing, and his claim to be here to write a book is probably bogus. I have little doubt that Mercer is Faber.'

'As little doubt as when you assured me Dale was Faber?'

Alvarez did not try to answer.

'Because my mind was occupied by matters of far greater importance than this absurd request from England, I failed to remember that where you are, there is chaos. I doubt you have the capacity to recognize even half the harm your incompetence has so nearly caused. The English would have laughed at our ineptitude; you would have impugned the honour of the Cuerpo.'

'I did advise you against telling England anything before further enquiries were made and—'

'You did no such thing.'

'Señor, I said—'

'You said nothing. During my banishment to this island, I have found nothing more disturbing than the inability of anyone to tell the truth, whether it is a farmer's wife trying to sell a caterpillar-eaten lettuce from a market stall or an inspector trying to blame others for his own bungling ineptitude.' He slammed down the receiver.

Alvarez rang the bell. After a while Susan appeared around the corner of Villa Bellavista and, when she recognized him, smiled. 'That man again! So what's the attraction this time?'

Her minimal bikini. 'I'm hoping Señor Mercer has returned from Palma.'

'He did, earlier, but then went off again with Dick to look at a house. I'm here because I'm off work and Steve said we could swim whenever we wanted. The beaches have become so crowded that even the Germans are having difficulty in finding spaces.'

'Have you any idea when they will be back?'

'Soon, I'd guess. So why not remain until they do. Or would that be boring?'

Women had strange ideas. 'Thank you, I'll stay.'

'Let's sit by the pool. And I can offer you a drink because Steve, bless his generosity, allows us to make reasonable use of the cellar.'

He followed her along the gravel path to the small swimming pool, bordered on two sides by a lantana hedge. She walked with grace. As he had noted before, her legs were long and slender. The bikini was just tight enough to testify her buttocks were firm and shapely . . . He cursed his mind. Why could he not restrict his interest to the hibiscus bushes which were flowering in such profusion?

Three chairs were set around a small patio table, in the centre of which was set a sun umbrella. 'What would you like to drink?' she asked.

'May I have a *coñac* with ice?'

'You've no desire to experiment?'

Not a question to answer.

She smiled, went into the small pool-house – little more than a wooden shed – in which were a pint-sized refrigerator and two shelves on which stood bottles and glasses. He stared across the pool at the visible portion of an almond tree and tried to think about almonds.

She returned, handed him a glass, sat. As she raised her glass, she said, 'May all our wishes come true.'

He drank. Her wishes were hardly likely to match his.

'I imagine you live nearby,' she said.

'In the village.'

'I love wandering around there. It's all so different. The little shops where people chat for minutes before buying anything; the narrow streets that twist and turn; the way, when it's really hot, people sit outside in the street and chat.'

'And every time another supermarket opens, several corner shops have to close.'

'Some have survived.'

'Very few and for how long?'

'It's happened everywhere. Would you wish to return to the past?'

'Which past?'

'How do you mean?'

'The past when there were many corner shops and no supermarkets, yes. But not the other past, before the tourists arrived, when there was little work except on the land, which was largely owned by the nobles or the church and peasants were ill paid; drought could bring near starvation; food was largely beans, cabbages, olives, oil, bread made from carob beans, and the very occasional treat like dried apricots; accommodation could be nothing more than a hut of wood and straw; there were diseases like cholera and millions of mosquitoes brought malaria; a doctor could be a long mule-cart journey away and his fees too great even for the dying.'

'Was it like that when you were young?'

'Things had begun to improve. But my father often spoke with such feeling, it became as if I had lived through such times.'

'The tourists changed everything?'

'Their money did.'

She began to trace a rough pattern on the frosting on her glass. 'I've heard people say tourism is a curse. But if it's done so much for the island, it can't be.'

'It has destroyed much that was bad; it has also destroyed much that was good. It has brought reformed houses, good water, drains, as much wholesome food as a man can eat, and a health service where one can consult a doctor even if one's pockets are empty. But it has tried to turn ancient fiestas into tourist attractions, destroyed natural beauty by burying it under concrete, taught the young to want everything now, and it has introduced drugs.'

'What a pleasure it would be to go with you and meet the real people, see the real island!'

If only she had not been married, he would have offered her that pleasure.

They heard the sound of a car's arriving, the slamming of doors. 'You haven't had very long to wait after all,' she said. 'For which, no doubt, you are grateful.'

He was, but only because Dolores had claimed a woman knew what a man was thinking. Although he did not believe that, he was worried there might be some truth in it and his thoughts, against his wish, had been growing ever warmer.

She called out, 'We're here.'

Mercer came in sight and walked up to where they sat. Alvarez stood, shook hands.

'I thought I recognized your car,' Mercer said. He looked at the glasses on the table. 'Good, Susan's offered hospitality which, like charity, begins at home. If you'll excuse me a moment, I'll pour myself a drink.' He went past them and into the pool-house.

Susan shouted, 'What was the place like?'

Mercer stepped out of the pool-house, empty glass in one hand. 'Small, badly sited, overpriced, and in need of very considerable restoration.' He returned inside.

'One more place he won't be buying,' she said.

'The señor is thinking of living here?'

'More a holiday home, I think.'

'Correct,' said Mercer as he stepped out of the pool-house and approached them. 'Like everyone else, after a couple of days in the sun I started dreaming of buying somewhere here. But also, no doubt like everyone else, I have been staggered by the price of property.' He moved a chair out of the edge of the shade into the full sun, sat. 'I will have to win the lottery before I can buy the kind of place I want.'

'You could try inland, señor,' Alvarez said. 'There, property is much cheaper.'

'Then what of my dream of sitting in a deckchair on a cloudless day, glass in hand, staring out at a millpond sea?' He drank. 'To sadder matters. Are you still searching for the girl?'

'We are, señor, but that is not why I am here.'

'No?'

'I am here to ask for your passport.'

'Good God! Why do you want that?'

'It is necessary for me to see it.'

'Why?'

'I am afraid I cannot explain.'

'Are you accusing me of something?'

'I am not accusing you of anything.'

'Then why d'you want my passport?'

'I can only repeat what I have just said.'

'Then I'm damned if—'

'Don't be silly, Steve,' she said.

'—I hand it over without any explanation?'

'The police get annoyed when foreigners try to be difficult.'

'In England . . .'

'You are in Spain.'

Alvarez said, 'If you would be kind enough to get it for me now, señor. I have a great deal more to do when I leave here.'

'You hardly seemed overworked when I arrived.'

'I had to wait for you to return.'

'The inspector's only doing his job,' Susan said hastily.

Mercer hesitated, put his glass down on the table, left. 'I'm afraid he hasn't totally dropped into the rhythm of the island,' she said. 'It must annoy you when foreigners complain because things are done differently here than in their home countries.'

'It can be annoying, but I try to understand.'

'As you've just shown.'

Thorne came round the house and up to where they sat. 'Good evening, Inspector.'

Alvarez returned the greeting.

He spoke to Susan. 'I wondered if the pool needed skimming before I pack up?'

'I don't think so,' she replied.

He stepped across to the edge of the pool and visually inspected it. 'I thought the light wind might have blown some leaves into it, but you're right. Since I'm here, I'll check the water.' He went into the pool-house, came out with a plastic test container and two bottles. He leaned over and filled the two tubes in the container with water, lifted it up, added drops from the bottles, checked the colours of the water, emptied it. 'Spot on . . . Is something up with Steve? He went past looking like he wanted to go fifteen rounds with someone.'

'He's furious because the inspector wants his passport.'

'Oh! Why?'

'Ask the inspector.'

'And no doubt receive a Delphic answer. I'll skip that . . . I'm off home for a shower. Are you returning soon?'

'Unless Steve decides he wants a nine-course dinner.'

'If so, prepare nine ham sandwiches. How about eating out tonight?'

'Why not?'

'We can try that new place in the port, one road back from the front. John reckons their *menu del dia* is the best value locally . . . See you back in the flat.' He said goodbye to Alvarez, left.

Alvarez was intrigued by the lack of warmth with which she had spoken to her husband. A sign of matrimonial differences? The result of the stresses following the move from one country to another, often the cause of trouble? But then he was forgetting that the English were notorious for preferring single bedrooms where their wives were concerned, double bedrooms where their mistresses were. The higher the male's social status, the more hunting, shooting and fishing provided his pleasures.

'You're very silent,' Susan said.

'I'm sorry.'

'Don't apologize. It's pleasant to be with a man who doesn't talk and talk to impress.'

Mercer returned, held out his passport.

'Thank you, señor.'

'How long are you going to keep it?'

'Only for a short time.'

'I hope that's right, since one can't do a damn thing without showing something to prove you are who you are.'

'Unfortunately, we have visitors who use false identities to steal.'

Mercer looked away. A guilty conscience, Alvarez thought, often found danger in words which to the innocent were innocuous. He stood. 'Thank you for your kindness, señora; thank you for you help, señor.'

She smiled as she said goodbye; Mercer did not.

He drove out on to the road and turned left; a kilometre on, he passed an old stone-built house which was being renovated. Mercer had been surprised by the cost of property. Andrés, who owned that house, would be delighted. When the renovation was complete, he would either sell it or rent it for a small fortune. Lucky the man who inherited property.

He joined a queue of four cars waiting to turn on to the main road, checked the time. The photographers would still be open, but to go there and explain what he wanted would take time. And what would be lost by waiting?

He drove home.

Unusually, the next morning Alvarez arrived at the post almost on time. The peace of the cloudless, sun-bright day was soon destroyed. The phone rang.

'I have just received a fax from England,' Salas said. 'With their usual bad manners, they wrote in English. I have had it translated. They ask if we have managed to make progress in tracing Faber. I am tempted to reply that we have not because you have been devoting your time and effort to investigating a man who clearly was not Faber.'

'Initially, there was reason to judge Dale might be Faber. Indeed, he still puzzles me, but I am convinced he is not and Mercer is.'

'A certainty until you next change your mind. Have you obtained a photograph of Mercer?'

'Yes, señor.'

'You will fax it to me now, together with your written report.'

'I can't.'

'Because you have, conforming to tradition, done nothing?'

'Because I have taken his passport to the photographers to have the photo reproduced.'

'You've done what? It escaped you that your action will have alerted him? Did it call for too much initiative to take a photo of him without his knowledge?'

'He will have been alerted long before I asked for his passport, since he will not have believed my explanation for asking the questions I did.'

'You saw no reason to provide an explanation he would believe?'

'I very much doubt I could have done so. If you're on the run . . .'

'How many times do I have to tell you that it is insulting to speak personally. You will speak impersonally.'

'If one is on the run, having committed a very large fraud, one is going to be suspicious of a policeman if he asks questions, whatever these are. Guilt sees danger everywhere. So on the assumption that my questioning must have alerted him, I decided to demand his passport, which meant he would be unable to flee the island while I gained a photo and a passport which can be checked with the English authorities to confirm it is false.'

There was a brief silence. 'Did you tell the photographers that this is priority?'

'Of course, señor.'

'You will get it to me the moment you receive it.' Salas rang off.

Alvarez decided to take the passport along to the photographers when he had had his *merienda*.

Alvarez awoke, summoned enough energy to check the time, found he could enjoy another five minutes' siesta. He stared up at the ceiling. For once, life was rewarding. Dolores had overcome her feminine stupidities and served a meal far superior to one or two they had recently been suffering – the *almejas en salsa verde* had been notable; she had made no comment when he had reached into the sideboard and brought out another bottle of wine; the children had been almost quiet; someone had given Jaime a bottle of Carlos I and Dolores had again remained silent when they replenished their glasses.

He went downstairs. The *coca* had been bought from a baker in the port who made it so light, it might have been made from moonbeams; the hot chocolate was rich. He drove to work to find someone drawing out of and freeing his favourite parking space, under the shade of a tree. No tourist annoyed him on his walk to the post. The duty *cabo* gave him a friendly greeting.

He slowly climbed the stairs, went through to his room, sat at the desk. He could understand the exalted mind of a seaman whose ship had survived a raging storm to reach the calm of harbour.

The phone rang: Raquel asking him if he would like to eat French for a change? *Poularde de Bresse en vessie*?

'Inspector Alvarez?'

The speaker was male and his voice held a hint of authority. Could life ever be more than fleetingly perfect? 'Speaking.'

'Gallardo, Mobile Reserves. There's been a vehicle accident on the Parelona road, six kilometres from Parelona. A Renault Clio, heading east, swerved off the road on a very tight corner and went over the edge. The driver, the only occupant, wasn't wearing his seat belt and was thrown out through the doorway . . .'

'Is he dead?'

'Have you often seen a man walking around after being impaled on the branch of a pine tree?'

'How am I supposed to know what happened to him?'

'By waiting for me to finish my report. As far as we can tell now, the driver came round the corner far too quickly, lost control, and went over—'

'Then it's a traffic accident and remains your concern, not mine.'

'There's a problem which is your concern. He has no identifying papers on him. Almost certainly a tourist since it's a hire car from Garajes Grandes in Port Llueso. We need you to contact the garage and find out who rented it.'

'If you phone them, they'll tell you.'

'Not our job.'

'Is anything?'

'The registration number is CKC 85336. Get back on to us as quick as you like.'

People, he thought sourly as he replaced the receiver, were becoming ever more eager to avoid work. He dialled the car-hire firm, spoke to one of the mechanics.

'Is the car a total?'

'I haven't seen it, but it sounds very likely.'

'That'll make the boss curse.'

'When it's insured for more than it's worth?'

'You lot have black minds. Hang on and I'll check the records.'

Alvarez slumped back in the chair, his mood now far from euphoric. 'In the midst of life we are in death.' No matter if one had led a blameless life, had devoted onself to others, one was going to die. He was going to die because he had lived.

'Are you there?'

'Yes.' But for how long?

'The hirer was an Englishman. Steven Mercer.'

Twelve

'The superior chief is engaged so you will ring later,' the plum-voiced secretary said.

Alvarez looked at his watch. It was already well past five. 'Would you tell him it is important.'

'One does not interrupt the superior chief unless there is an emergency.'

'But it is very important.'

There was silence. Then Salas said, 'What?'

'I have to report a vehicle accident, señor, in which—'

'I am at a very important meeting. When I was informed you wished to speak to me concerning an emergency—'

'I didn't say that.'

'—having apologized to the other persons present – an unwelcome obligation considering who one of them is – I leave the room and discover the emergency is a mere traffic accident. I have an inspector who, incredible as it must seem, has not yet learned that that is a matter for the mobile unit or Trafico.'

'I do know that, but—'

'It becomes ever clearer you know little or nothing.' The line went dead.

Alvarez fiddled the itching lobe of his right ear where a mosquito had stung it. Were Salas's words authority for taking no further interest in the matter? He would have liked to think so, but couldn't. He dialled Palma.

'Who is it?' the secretary demanded.

'Inspector Alvarez. I must speak to Señor Salas.'

'You were unable to understand how annoyed the superior chief was at being disturbed for no valid reason?'

Her lofty scorn annoyed him even more than usual. 'He'll be even more annoyed if you haven't the sense to appreciate I must speak to him.'

'Wait.'

That single word had been encased in ice. Glumly he accepted he should not have allowed his annoyance to surface. Being a woman, she would not forget; she would resentfully recall his words whenever there was a chance to denigrate him to Salas.

'Are you drunk?' Salas demanded.

'No, señor.'

'Then you are guilty of a stupidity which is remarkable by any standard, even yours.'

'Señor, when I said—'

'Or is your seeming stupidity once again a mask?'

'When I said—'

'A mask concealing a deliberate attempt to cause me the utmost annoyance.'

'I was about to tell you why the traffic accident was so important when the line went dead. It is sufficiently important to disturb you even though it is not, strictly speaking, an emergency.'

'You are admitting you had no right to tell my secretary it was?'

'I didn't. I said the matter was very important.'

'I prefer to believe her.'

'I will visually identify the victim, of course, but since the car was hired in his name, I don't imagine there can be much doubt . . .'

'When you speak, there is always doubt. What the devil are you trying to tell me?'

'The car had been hired by Mercer. You may remember

he was the man I have provisionally identified as Faber . . .'

'Is your insolence without limits?'

'Why do you ask that, señor?'

'You can ask?'

There was a silence.

'Well?' Salas said angrily.

'Señor, I am a little uncertain as to who is asking what.'

'It is grossly insulting to suggest your senior officer does not remember a vital point of the case.'

'But I didn't.'

'"May" does not suggest doubt?'

'What "may"?'

'If this continues, I shall be in no fit state to return to the meeting. You will tell me what you have to say and ring off.'

'But I have, señor.'

The line went dead. Alvarez slowly replaced the receiver. He stared through the unshuttered window at the wall of the building on the opposite side of the road. Perhaps Salas lacked the mental capacity to consider at the same time the consequences of Mercer's death and whatever was the subject of the meeting he was attending. He had given no indication of appreciating that when the dead man was identified as Faber, the case would be closed and the English must admire the Cuerpo's sharp efficiency. Justice demanded he receive praise for solving the case. Unfortunately, justice, like wealth, was seldom granted to the deserving.

He poured himself a drink. Tomorrow was Thursday and he would be dining with Raquel. Would the meal be as delicious as on the previous occasion, the wine as grand? Any woman who could cook as she did was a treasure – even as a wife. Youth inevitably attracted, but maturity could possess charm. Sa Echona now had perhaps a hundred and fifty hectares; the soil was rich and almost free of rocks, thanks to generations of peasants who had lifted them and used them to make walls; it could grow anything a man might reasonably desire. On the island, a woman's wealth did not automatically become her husband's on marriage, but a man could learn to live with that.

Years before, there had been no attempt to camouflage the mortuary – better to accept death when poor – but in recent years, prosperity had introduced a greater sensitivity. It had been moved and was now a rock-built house with an extension behind. Ironically, the next house was owned by a midwife. Alvarez walked ever more slowly. There were many aspects of his job he disliked; viewing death topped the list. To look at a dead person was to see one's future.

He stepped into Reception, once the *entrada*. There were artistically arranged fresh flowers, two paintings depicting ascents to heaven, three chairs, and a small table on which were pamphlets entitled 'To meet the life beyond without pain'; these detailed the undertaker's costs.

Venegas entered and shook hands. 'Not seen you here for a while.'

And if it were twice as long before the next time, he would be grateful.

'How's Dolores?'

'Fine.'

'Ordering Jaime around?'

'Sometimes.'

'You're in a talkative mood!' Venegas laughed. 'Scared one of the ladies in the freezer will wake up and remind you of your past?'

'I am in a bit of a rush, so if we could hurry it up?'

Venegas's tone became sour. 'They say, give a man a

touch of authority and he thinks himself governor-general. Then I will hurry it up, Governor-General.'

The extension behind the house, on what had once been garden, had no windows and the practical ugliness of a typical supermarket. Inside was tiled cleanliness and powerful air-conditioning kept the atmosphere pleasant. In the centre was a tilting examination table above which was a pod of lights; against the walls were six refrigerated compartments, dual stainless-steel sinks, sterilizing cabinet, and store cupboard.

'He's well messed up,' Venegas said, as he gripped the handle of the top, right-hand cabinet.

'All I need to see is the face.'

He pulled the compartment out, describing the injuries in detail as he did so. Alvarez tried not to listen, certain he was being mocked.

Venegas folded back the white cover to expose face and shoulders.

Alvarez said, 'It's Mercer.'

'That's all you want?'

'Yes.'

'So what happens now?'

'I can't be certain.'

'I need to know.'

'Worried about being paid?' Alvarez asked, glad to have the opportunity to remind the other of his reputation as a skinflint.

As he drove to Villa Bellavista, Alvarez tried to judge how the Thornes would receive the news. It would not be with the bitter grief he sometimes faced which distressed him for days: Mercer was not a close relative but merely, indirectly, their temporary employer with whom they had become friendly. Yet it was sad to lose even a casual friend and the circumstances of Mercer's death would probably increase that sadness.

He parked, climbed out of the Ibiza, crossed the gravel drive to the front door and rang the bell. Susan opened the door.

'We'll soon have to give you a key!' She became uneasy when he did not respond. 'Do . . . do you want to come in?'

He stepped inside, followed her to the rear patio where chairs were set around a table in the shade. 'Is your husband here?'

'He's working at one of the places in Bernejo, tidying up after the last lot of tourists – he says the place has been left like a rubbish dump. It is extraordinary how some people behave on holiday. But perhaps some of them live like that at home . . . What would you like to drink – the usual?'

'Thank you, I won't have anything.'

'You're not yourself. Is something wrong?'

'I'm afraid I have some bad news.'

'Not . . . not Dick?'

'It's nothing to do with him.'

'Thank God!'

'Señor Mercer has had a very serious car accident. Sadly, he died in it.'

She sat. 'It's impossible! He left here . . . Christ! it pulls you up short when you chat to someone before he drives off and then you learn he won't be returning because he's dead. I feel . . .' She stood, hurried into the house.

He stared at the pool and watched the very slight movement of the surface water as it responded to the breeze and reflected the sun's rays in sharp bursts.

She returned, her eyes reddened. 'It's such a shock.'

'Would you like me to find your husband?'

She shook her head. 'I'm all right. It was just the suddenness.'

'Is there anything I can do for you?'

'I don't think so.'

'Then I'll leave.'

'You've been so understanding.'

'I hope I have been,' he said before he turned and left.

Alvarez was about to enter the post on Thursday when he remembered he had not collected the photograph of Mercer. He continued on to the old square, the large part of which was raised to ensure it was level. Scaffolding was being erected for the coming exhibition of Mallorquin dancing. Dolores would insist both Jaime and he accompany her and the children to watch it. He would plead work.

The show windows of any photographer were clear evidence of the level of present prosperity; a few of the cameras bore price tags in hundreds of euros, yet when he had been young, even a simple box camera would have been beyond the means of all but a handful. He went in and spoke to one of the assistants, collected two copy photographs and the passport.

To return to the post, he passed through the square once more. As used to be said, 'If acorns are lying under an oak tree, pick them up and eat them.' Never pass up an opportunity. He went into Club Llueso and had a drink.

Alvarez waited until he was peeling an apple to say, 'By the way, I won't be here for supper.'

'Indeed,' Dolores remarked.

'I thought I'd let you know in good time.'

'It is surprising you should bother.' She ate a segment of orange. 'It seems foreign women lack a sense of humour as well as shame.'

'Why say that?' Jaime asked.

'It is not obvious? To see an old man behaving as if he were twenty again would cause any decent Mallorquin woman to laugh with contempt.'

Alvarez sliced right through a quarter of apple instead of, as intended, just deep enough to remove the core. 'I am not an old man and I am not going out with a young foreign woman.' He wondered why he continued to deny? People refused the truth if it contradicted what they were pleased to believe.

'It's good to see you again,' Raquel said, as he entered the smaller sitting room.

'It's great to be here.'

'Sit down and tell me what you'd like to drink.'

'May I have a *coñac*?'

'With just ice?' She smiled, turned and spoke to Margarita, who had remained in the doorway. 'And I'll have a Dubonnet. And don't forget a slice of lemon.'

Margarita disappeared.

'Have you been busy, Enrique?'

'Very busy.'

'But hopefully not because of more silly women forgetting where they've put their jewellery?'

'If you hadn't forgotten, I wouldn't be here.'

'And that makes up for everything?'

'More than.'

'It's such a pleasure to talk to a man who knows how to be gallant. Most Mallorquins haven't even heard the word.'

He felt a little taller and a little thinner.

'I've been busy too. Trying to work out how best to manage the estate. It's such a difficult decision. Uncle Eduardo ran it on traditional lines because he lived in the past and I'm sure that's what he'd want me to do. But is that possible with costs so high because of the euro?'

'It's impossible to farm now as it was even thirty years ago, because of not only the cost, but also the lack of men ready to do the work. Modernize completely, for instance, rip out trees so that the fields can be easily ploughed by a large tractor, and with luck you'll make a small profit – not a generous one because no government, except the French, encourages farmers. But that will mean the character of the estate will change. Yet if there isn't change, there's stagnation. So it's a case of modernizing realistically. Perhaps most importantly, note what crops are imported that can be grown here and work out which will be the most profitable; try some of the more exotic fruits and vegetables. Run sheep once more, importing rams that will make for more solid carcasses – Suffolk is a good breed; build lambing sheds to cut losses and races to hold animals when a vet regularly examines them. This all costs and many would tell you it's a ridiculous extravagance, but healthier sheep mean better lambs which make more money which gradually replaces capital . . . I'm sorry, I'm boring you.'

'You most certainly are not. I'd no idea quite how interested you are in farming. If only there were someone like you . . .' She did not finish.

To manage the estate whilst warming her heart?

'Your glass is empty. You will have another, won't you? I like a man who enjoys his drink.'

Clearly, she and Dolores would still disagree about many things.

When he drove away from Sa Echona, his mind was crowded. The meal. The largest *gambas* he could remember seeing, let alone eating. *Cordero al chilidron*. The lamb as tender as a virgin's smile, the sauce as tasty as a virgin's kiss. *Helado de crema Catalana*. Not an ice cream he had enjoyed before, but one he hoped to do so again soon. Marqués de Murrieta Castillo Ygay, as smooth as silk. Ryst VSOP, the first armagnac he had drunk for a long while and one to shake his reverence for cognac . . .

She had not hidden her admiration for his suggested

improvement to the estate. He was surer now about what she would have said, had she finished the sentence, 'If only there were someone like you . . .'

Thirteen

As Alvarez settled behind his desk, the phone rang. He stared at it with uneasy annoyance. Who would be phoning so early in the morning? Unfortunately, he would have to find out.

'So you have finally decided to arrive and do a little work,' Salas said sarcastically.

He looked up at the clock on the wall, but that had stopped some time ago; he could never remember to buy new batteries. He looked at his watch and was surprised. So that was why Dolores had vexatiously urged him to hurry! 'Señor, I urgently needed to have a word with a man who might have been able to help me in one of the many cases I must work on and, since he lives on my route to the post, I thought it better to stop and talk to him rather than drive straight here, since that would later require me to go there and back again. As you have often said, for a detective, a minute saved can be worth an hour.'

'But in some cases, not worth the saving . . . I have just heard from England.'

'That's quick.'

'By some standards.'

'Do they express their appreciation of our work, señor?'

'I suppose you could say they do.'

'That's good.'

'You think an appreciation is always to be welcomed?'

'But why not?'

'Because it may well be, and in this case is, adverse.'

'I don't understand.'

'A circumstance with which you will be very familiar. Alvarez, you have made a fool of yourself and a laughing stock of the Cuerpo.'

'How?'

'You misled me into believing Dale was Faber. I forwarded this opinion to England. It was, of course, nonsense. Then you said that, beyond question, Mercer was Faber. Again, because of the pressure of work, I did not accept your claim was bound to be further nonsense and I again forwarded it to England. As a result, the English will now smile sarcastically whenever they think of us. Even a half-witted Galician could not have brought more shame to the Cuerpo.'

'But why?'

'Because a half-wit is not as damaging as someone with no wit at all.'

'Señor, why should the English regard us with anything but admiration when we have, after a slight hesitation, successfully completed a task which you originally referred to as ridiculous because it was impossible?'

'I did no such thing. And, even after all these years, your obtuseness has the capacity to astonish me. You are quite unable to understand why the English police must now regard us with amused scorn since we pointed out that we quickly succeeded where they had failed.'

'I never wrote anything like that.'

'I added a comment to your report.'

'Then you can hardly blame me . . .'

'It was your stupidity which caused me to write it.'

'True I came to a wrong conclusion about Dale, but I soon corrected that . . .'

'And made another absurd identification.'

'Did what?'

'You do not understand your own language?'

'You seem to be suggesting my identification of Faber was wrong.'

'Seem to be? Are you incapable of rational speech? I told you, the English have taken great pleasure in informing us that Mercer was not Faber.'

'But . . . And you didn't . . .'

'Didn't what?'

'Tell me, señor. And I can't believe he wasn't Faber.'

'A fool will believe anything.'

'If he wasn't Faber, why did he lie over things which could be of no account unless he was? He claimed he'd worked in an agriculture firm. He'd told the staff he worked in computing. Why lie about that unless trying to hide his skill at a computer? He said he'd been left money, given up his job and come to the island to write. The staff said he never did any work. The facts all point to one thing: he was Faber. Did you send the photograph of him together with the written report?'

'You would suggest I am as incompetent as you? Rest assured that the next time I speak to the Director-General, I will observe that, in my opinion, you have never been a suitable member of the Cuerpo.' He rang off.

Alvarez replaced the receiver. He opened the bottom right-hand drawer of the desk.

'Uncle Enrique looks like he's swallowed a toad,' Juan said.

'That's rude.' Isabel giggled.

'And stupid,' Dolores said. 'Juan, if you can't learn good manners, you'll eat your meals in the kitchen.'

'So I won't have to see all the disgusting food in his mouth when he eats with it wide open,' Isabel said.

'I don't.'

'You do.'

'No, I bloody well don't.'

'How dare you speak such language,' Dolores said angrily.

'It wasn't bad. I didn't say—'

'And you will not say it now. Have you both finished eating?'

They had.

'I want you to leave for school at a quarter to.'

'That's too soon,' Juan complained.

'I think not, since you were late yesterday.'

'The chain on my bicycle slipped and I had to get it back on.'

'What have I said to you about lying?'

'But it did slip.'

'On another day. You were late yesterday because you met Jorge on the way and tried riding his new bike.'

'How . . . how do you know that?'

'A mother knows far more than her children believe she does.'

'Isabel sneaked on me.'

'I did not,' Isabel said loudly.

'Yes you did.'

'Isabel made no mention of the incident yesterday,' Dolores said firmly. 'You can both get down now and you will make certain you arrive at school on time.'

They hurried out of the room.

'You tell him off for lying,' Jaime said, 'and then you lie to him.'

'I most certainly did not.'

'I heard Isabel telling you what had happened, yet you've just said she didn't.'

'I said she made no mention of it yesterday. She told me this morning.'

'That's quibbling.'

'It is bringing up children to tell the truth.' She began to collect up the plates.

'By not telling it?'

'If I explain, you will not understand.'

Jaime reached for the bottle of Soberano.

'You have had enough,' she snapped.

He withdrew his hand.

'You can bring the glasses out to the kitchen.'

Alvarez watched Jaime stand. Would he never learn a woman had to be humoured, not challenged? The phone rang. The call had to be for either Dolores or Jaime. He was about to pick up the bottle to refill his glass when Dolores came through the bead curtain and continued through to the *entrada*.

He refilled his glass, hurriedly replaced the bottle when he heard her return.

'It's for you,' she said. 'That woman.'

'Salas's secretary?'

'Raquel.' She stood with her arms folded across her breast, her expression combative.

'What's she want?' he asked, before accepting that in the circumstances, it was not the most sensible of questions.

'For you to see her again.'

'Has she lost something more?'

'If so, tell her to look for it herself.'

'If I did that, she'd complain officially and I'd be in right royal trouble.'

'As my mother used to say, "A man speaks bravely until it is time to act."'

He went through to the *entrada* and, after closing the door, picked up the receiver. 'Good afternoon.'

'I hope I haven't upset Dolores? She sounded rather grim when I told her who I was.'

'She's not feeling too well.'

'One of the perils of growing old. I hope you enjoyed last night?'

'Very much.'

'You didn't find my cooking disappointing after Dolores's?'

'Quite the opposite.'

'I'm so glad. I want to ask a question. I hope you don't mind?'

She had spoken archly, as might a woman who wanted to attract a man without being too obvious.

'Of course I don't.'

'Rafael has actually shown some initiative and suggested we rip out the old fig trees and replace them with algorobbas; these days no one can be bothered to harvest figs and sun-dry them because that's such a long and boring job. But I like the trees, especially in winter when the leafless branches look like grasping fingers.'

That seemed a strange reason for preserving fig trees; a lubricious reason if one remembered on the island 'fig' had the double meaning.

'I expect you like figs when they're ripe?'

He shocked himself by wondering if she had a far more earthy sense of humour than he would have judged.

'I musn't keep you, but when you have the time, let me know what you think I should do about the trees.'

'Yes, of course.'

'You're not very talkative.'

'I've a slight sore throat.'

'From eating too many figs?' She laughed. 'Suppose you come here to dinner tomorrow and you give me your thoughts?'

'That would be fine.'

'You're certain? You're not worried about what Dolores will have to say about your coming here again so soon?'

'Of course not.'

'I'm only teasing. You obviously lead your own life, as any real man does. So I'll say goodbye until then.'

He replaced the receiver, his thoughts scrambled. The dining room was empty, but as he crossed to the table to pick up his glass, Dolores entered from the kitchen. 'I began to think you must have gone upstairs for your siesta.' She obviously knew he had not. 'Has she lost her jewellery again?'

'No.'

'Yet you found much to talk about. Surprising, since one of the teachers said she had the intelligence of a donkey. What did she want?'

'Some advice on trees.'

'She believes you are an expert?'

'She just wanted an opinion.'

'From you, when she could tell the foremost arboriculturist to visit her? Enrique, have I not explained what kind of a woman she is?'

'You've been more than critical of her. Maybe you two didn't get on well when you were young . . .'

'Young or old, one does not become friendly with someone who has the character of a viper. Unless, of course, one is determined to be blind . . . You must understand, I do not want to see you hurt.'

'She may attack me?'

'I may well attack you if you continue to talk stupidly. She is friendly only if there is a reason to be.'

'I think you're misjudging her. And I can't say she's all that friendly.'

'Then why does she phone you for an hour?'

'It was ten minutes at the most. And I had to calm her down.'

'She became so excited about the trees?'

'She thinks there may have been an attempted burglary. I convinced her, from what she told me, that that seemed unlikely, but said I would call in when I've a moment to spare. She's a nervous woman living on her own and it will be good public relations to show willing.'

'She has no staff despite the size of her palace?'

'There's Margarita the housekeeper, and a gardener, but I don't think there's anyone else who's permanently employed. Of course, she probably has a couple of women who come in to do much of the cleaning . . .'

'If she has a housekeeper, she is not alone. To call her nervous is to exaggerate beyond reason. She has lost nothing, yet has to be calmed down by an hour's soothing?'

'It's the thought of what might have been which can be so upsetting.'

'It is the thought of what likely will be that upsets me, but what can I do? One can talk to a man, but one cannot make him listen.' She marched back into the kitchen.

Fourteen

Saturday should have been a day of relaxation since ideally work stopped at midday and did not resume until Monday. But this Saturday Alvarez was too worried to relax. Dolores suspected he was becoming friendly with Raquel. He had done his best to assure her this was ridiculous, but she was not a woman who readily allowed her mind to be changed. And should she learn that her suspicions were justified, she would serve meals not fit for a beggar. Then there was the problem of Mercer. If he were not Faber, who and where was Faber? As he had maintained from the beginning, an impossible question for the Cuerpo to answer. Salas should inform England that it could now be stated Faber was not living in Llueso or the surrounding area under an assumed name. But Salas could not be relied upon to do the sensible thing. There was every chance the investigation would continue, calling for endless work trying to solve the insoluble.

The phone interrupted his gloomy thoughts.

'Rosello here, Institute of Forensic Anatomy. The report on the blood taken from Steven Mercer after death gives a hundred and seventy milligrams per one hundred millilitres of blood.'

'What does that mean in layman's terms?'

'He'll have been suffering a serious lack of judgement and caution.'

'He was too tight to drive a car?'

'To tight to be driving a car.'

'Then that explains the crash.'

'Perhaps.'

'Don't you blokes ever provide a definitive answer?'

'Not if we can avoid doing so, since that leaves the gate open if we turn out to be wrong.'

Alvarez thanked him, said goodbye, replaced the receiver. The phone rang. Did no one realize it was Saturday?

'Vehicles. Is that you, Enrique?'

'It is.'

'Eusebio here. How's the family?'

It was ten minutes before Nicolau explained the reason for the call. 'As you know, we examine every car involved in a major accident and try to determine the cause of the crash, so we've been working on the Renault Clio which belonged to Steven Mercer . . .'

'I could have saved you a whole load of trouble.'

'How so?'

'I've just received the lab report on Mercer's blood. He was well over the limit and so likely wasn't even aware of the bend until it was too late.'

'There's more to it than a drunken driver.'

Alvarez experienced sudden apprehension.

'The hydraulic system had been sabotaged. The brake line had been weakened so that it would give way under heavy braking.'

'That's . . . Couldn't it have been wear and tear, lack of servicing?'

'No.'

'How can you be so definite?'

'Because it's my job to be.'

'But perhaps you could be mistaken?'

'Do I tell you you're an incompetent detective? So don't try to tell me I'm an incompetent engineer.'

'I'm not. But what you're saying means someone deliberately engineered the crash. And driving to Parelona, tight, with all those dangerous bends, it was going to be a fatal crash. You're calling it murder.'

'I'm telling you what we found. It's up to you to decide whether it was murder or a drunken accident.'

'How can it be an accident if the brake line was sabotaged? Or are you saying it might have been done as a joke, not realizing the possible consequences?'

'Anyone doing that sort of thing as a joke has feathers between his ears. What is it with you? Trying to make things easy for someone?'

'That's a filthy suggestion.'

'You've been putting some to me which haven't gone down well.'

'I'm sorry, Eusebio, but things have become impossible. God knows what Salas will say when I tell him.'

'Then you're about find out.'

'That's hardly sympathetic.'

'I was up twice during the night because the latest is teething and it took me ages each time to get back to sleep; Águeda was feeling rotten so I had to get my own breakfast; the car wouldn't start for an age and it'll have to go to the garage, and they've racked up their charges until one has to be a millionaire to pay them; my boss has toothache and is more of a bastard than ever; and you expect me to be full of sympathy?'

'Sorry to hear all that. Life can get bloody.'

'I can bear it just as long as it's even more bloody for someone else.'

After ringing off, Alvarez tried, and failed, to think of a valid reason for not phoning Salas.

'Yes?' said the secretary.

'Inspector Alvarez from Llueso.'

'What do you want?'

A touch of friendly politeness would have made a start. 'I need to speak to the superior chief.'

'He is not available.'

'It's important.'

'Another emergency?'

'I never said it was an emergency . . .'

'I am to disbelieve my own ears?'

'Perhaps there was a misunderstanding . . .'

'Not on my part.'

'Señor Salas is working today?'

'Is there a reason why he should not be?'

'It is Saturday.'

'To someone who is dedicated to his work, that is of no importance.'

Dedication was a dangerous phenomenon. 'When can I speak to him?'

'I am unable to answer.'

'There's no knowing when he'll chip on to the nineteenth green?'

'You are trying to be humorous?'

He was being stupid. She would report that remark to Salas. 'I'll ring again later.'

'I will inform the superior chief that you have reported an emergency.'

He wondered if she was trying to be humorous or vindictive? He sighed. On top of all his other problems, he would now have to remain in the office until Salas phoned him or he phoned Palma and found Salas in his office.

Salas rang at a quarter to one, only minutes before Alvarez would have had to leave the office in order to enjoy a drink before lunch.

'What the devil is it this time?'

'Señor, I have received reports from the Institute of Forensic Anatomy and Vehicles.'

'Well?'

'The level of alcohol in the blood was high. Rosello, at the Institute, described it in practical terms as causing a serious loss of judgement and caution.'

'Who are you talking about?'

'Mercer.'

'Why are you incapable of making an efficient report by first identifying the person concerned?'

'I thought you must realize whom I was talking about.'

'I am not a cryptologist.'

'Yet since I am not dealing with any other death at the moment, the Institute could only be concerned with—'

'Do you intend to tell me what the reports are?'

'Mercer was too intoxicated to be driving a car. Learning this, I naturally assumed that this was the cause of the crash. Even sober, the drive to Parelona is dangerous—'

'Ridiculous!'

'Some of the corners are extremely sharp and beyond them are drops of hundreds of metres . . .'

'Fifty at the most.'

'It seems like hundreds if one suffers from altophobia.'

'A complaint solely in the mind.'

'Is that not where all complaints start?'

'A broken leg starts in the mind?'

'The pain does and it is the pain which is complained about. And if the person has to rely on only one leg—'

'You are supposed to be reporting on a fatal car crash, yet concern yourself with the seat of pain and legs. Have you recently consulted a psychiatrist?'

'I have never done so, señor.'

'An omission which should be rectified at the earliest possible moment. Perhaps we could return to the subject of the crash?'

'When I learned Mercer had been drinking heavily, I

assumed this to be the cause of the crash. To drive to Parelona when sober is fraught with danger—'

'Cease this absurdity.'

'Vehicles reported one of the hydraulic brake lines had been tampered with. Their expression was "sabotaged". I suggested the possibility of damage through lack of maintenance, but they were certain this had been occasioned deliberately.'

There was a long silence, which Salas ended. 'You do realize what you are saying?'

'It's Vehicles who said—'

'You have already complicated matters beyond measure by repeatedly proclaiming emergencies when there was none—'

'Señor, I said the matter was urgent, not an emergency.'

'And confusion has been your sole accomplishment. England made a ridiculous request, but because the Cuerpo does not acknowledge the word "impossible", we endeavoured to assist them. You chose to assume you had succeeded. Naturally, you were wrong. The manner in which you boasted about your achievement besmirched the honour of the Cuerpo. Now you introduce the murder of the man you stupidly named as Faber to add to the confusion. It would be no surprise to learn you are the guilty man, bringing even greater discredit to the Cuerpo.'

'That is a monstrous suggestion, señor.'

'What is the motive for this murder?'

'I do not know.'

'Why not?'

'It has only just become clear that the death of Mercer was murder.'

'Even a suspicion of initiative would have alerted you.'

'How could I suspect anything before Vehicles had examined the car and given me their findings?'

'Does this mean you have not yet started an investigation?'

'But if—'

'Perhaps you have not even considered the necessity of one?'

'I have decided that the first thing to do is to try to discover—'

'Do you always start an investigation by accepting the possibility of failure?'

'In the circumstances, it's going to be difficult and will take time to—'

'It is unnecessary to point that out since you are in charge of the case.'

'Motive is likely the key which opens the lock . . .'

'Refrain from such fanciful expressions.'

'If Mercer was Faber, the likely motive for his murder has to be connected with the theft . . .'

'Since Mercer was not Faber, your speculation is a waste of time.'

'I'll talk to the couple again who looked after the property he rented, since they may well have learned something that will provide a lead.'

'And if they can't?'

'Then I'll talk to other foreigners who knew him.'

'And if they can't?'

'Señor, have you not just said it is wrong to presume failure?'

'I despair of your ever understanding what is required of a good investigator.' Salas ended the conversation.

There were those who decried *bacalao* with reason; salt cod could be less than delicious. There were many who refused to eat *garbanzos*; chick peas could be a tasteless mush. There were even those who rejected *puerros*; leeks were not to everyone's taste. But put the three together in a soup cooked by Dolores (she added olive oil, onion, carrots, parsley, potatoes, garlic, bread, pepper and salt) and there was a dish no king would refuse.

After finishing his second helping, Alvarez said, 'I have now tasted perfection.'

Dolores looked at him briefly, her expression sharp. She stood. 'Pass your plate.'

She carried the dirty plates through to the kitchen. Jaime and Alvarez refilled their glasses with wine. She returned with a tray on which were three small earthenware dishes. 'I decided it would be nice to have *crema Catalana*.'

'Why?' Jaime asked.

'Does one have to have a reason?'

'You don't usually make a sweet.'

'And that is reason for not having one now?' She passed a small dish to each of them, then sat. 'I hope Isabel and Juan are behaving themselves.'

'I doubt it,' Jaime said.

'Why?'

'They seldom do.'

'That is a disgraceful thing to say. And if they do misbehave, do you know why?'

Alvarez dug his spoon through the caramelized top. It was so typical of life: he had praised the soup in order to ensure Dolores was in a good temper, and Jaime annoyed her.

'It is,' she said, snapping short each word, 'because of the example their father sets.'

'That's not right.'

'I am glad you are still capable of appreciating the fact.'

'I mean, it's wrong to say I set a bad example.'

'The young should be encouraged to speak crudely, swear, drink, leave everything to be done tomorrow because tomorrow never arrives?'

'That's not fair.'

'The truth seldom is.'

Alvarez finished eating. He wondered whether it was wise to have a brandy first – there were times when a man needed something extra – but decided it was not. He cleared his throat, spoke to Dolores. 'By the way, you won't be cooking anything special tonight, will you, not after a wonderful lunch?'

'Which took all morning to prepare, but there is nothing unusual in that. Yet, sadly, my husband questions why I bother to cook. Perhaps he considers the food he eats is not worth the effort of preparing it.'

'It is worth every single moment. This *crema Catalana* is a miracle.' He cleared his throat again. 'About supper?'

'What about it?'

'You will not be cooking anything special?'

'You expect me to spend the rest of the day slaving in the kitchen?'

'Of course not.'

'Then why do you ask?'

'I just wanted to make certain.'

'That it would not matter you would not be here for supper?'

'How . . .' He stopped.

'How do I know that? You think I did not understand why you praised the meal so fulsomely.'

'I spoke the truth.'

'But not because it was the truth.'

'What d'you mean by that?' Jaime asked.

She ignored him. 'In truth, any meal I cook has for you become no more than tourist food. When one can dine on lobster, mussels have little attraction.'

'I am not seeing her.'

'Who?' Jaime asked.

She again ignored him. 'You expect me to believe you?'

It seemed a woman might be able correctly to judge when a man was lying; but would her skill extend to appreciating that the lie was itself a lie when he admitted to something he had always vehemently denied? 'All right, if you must know, I'm seeing Fiona.'

'A foreign woman, young enough to be your granddaughter?'

'I doubt that.'

'Because you daren't accept it, since that must face you with the absurdity of chasing after young women who have only to look at you to remember their childhood.'

'Why do you keep saying I'm old?'

'You would have me mock the facts?' She stood. 'Having slaved all morning, fool that I am, I am now going to rest. You will clear the table, stacking everything clearly on the draining board.'

They watched her climb the stairs.

'She's never before left us to clear the table,' Jaime said in an aggrieved voice. 'It's a woman's job.'

'With Dolores upstairs and Isabel out, it's become a man's job. Think on the bright side: after we've done it, we can sit and pour a *coñac* and she won't be here to object.'

Minutes later, they gave themselves generous brandies. Jaime drank, put his glass down on the table, leaned forward. 'Is this Fiona one of the sisters?'

'That's right.'

'You're not seeing both of 'em together?'

'I thought it better if Dolores didn't know that. She's easily upset.'

'What do they see in you?'

'Passion unending.'

'You don't deserve to be such a lucky sod,' Jaime said bad-temperedly.

Raquel met Alvarez at the front door of Sa Echona. 'I wondered if you'd like to spend a little time looking around the grounds as well as at the fig trees?'

'Very much,' he answered. Her manner made it reasonably clear she had either forgotten or never known the double meaning.

'You must tell me what you'd do to improve absolutely everything. The only idea Rafael has had since I came here was the one I told you about on the phone. Unlike you, he simply can't understand that everything has to change all the time. Let's go down this side of the house.'

Old Eduardo had become interested in gardening – softening of the brain had been the general verdict – so there were many flower beds and an extensive lawn. To keep all this in order required much time and effort. The plants needed rooting out, the ground being either used for growing something useful or replanted with shrubs which needed little attention and no water. But would she accept that? Women seemed to gain some strange pleasure from flowers.

They stepped into the first of two greenhouses, battered by time and neglect but not yet beyond repair.

'I had a phone call from Ricardo this morning,' she said casually. 'I met him in Paris when I was married to Benoît. A mutual friend described him as suave, sophisticated, and socially dangerous. That was just about correct.' She laughed. 'He's on the island and suggested coming to a meal today. He was never backward in inviting himself.'

Then it was not going to be a tête-à-tête dinner, Alvarez thought despondently. The sophisticated newcomer would take one look at him and sneer at his clumsiness.

'I told him to come another day.'

He squared his shoulders. She had chosen an inspector in the Cuerpo over a socially dangerous and undoubtedly immensely rich Frenchman. He spoke even more enthusiastically about what he would do if the estate were his to cultivate.

Fifteen

Sunday was Sunday. Alvarez did not return to Villa Bellavista until Monday morning.

'Come in and tell me what's brought you here this time,' Susan said.

He followed her into the sitting room, admiring her neat figure as she walked ahead, sculptured yet concealed by the dressmaker's art. Was Dolores right? Not when she claimed he appeared old to the young, but when she said he was a fool to interest himself – in a purely platonic way, she could have added – in young foreign women. After all, they were unlikely to own many hectares of land.

'Would you like to be in or out?' she asked.

'It is pleasantly cool in here.'

'Then if you sit, I'll bring you a drink. The usual?'

'Thank you very much.'

He watched her leave. Brazilian men were said to regard a woman's buttocks as her great natural asset; they would find much to admire where Susan was concerned.

When she returned, Thorne was with her. He came ungracefully forward and shook hands. 'I'm taking a short coffee break, Inspector, so for once you find me at home. I suppose you're here because of the terrible accident?'

'That is so.'

'We've been told by the agency to collect up everything of his and take it to them. Is that all right by you?'

He was about to say yes – the wise man let others do

the work – but it occurred to him that Salas would ask if he had checked Mercer's papers. 'I'll have a look through them before they leave here.'

'Are they handy?' Thorne asked Susan.

'Everything he had is in the bedroom, on the bed.'

'Then I'd better have a quick check now,' Alvarez said.

'Before the drink I started to get you?' she asked.

He was glad she had not forgotten.

Twenty minutes later, he stepped into a bedroom with two single beds, a dressing table, a chair and a built-in cupboard. At the head of one bed, neatly arranged, were clothes; in the middle of it were various objects including a laptop computer, a couple of paperbacks and the passport he had returned; at the foot were a couple of typed pages, a folder on the front of which was printed 'Lesson Two: dialogue'. and a wallet. He picked up the top typed page and read. He was no literary critic, but it was obvious Mercer had had a long way to go before he could confidently have moved on to lesson three. The wallet contained two hundred and twenty euros. A cheque book had been issued by Sa Nostra. One of the paperbacks was subtitled 'Life in a mansion in the nineteenth century'. On Spanish television they had recently rerun *Upstairs, Downstairs* and he had wondered as he watched how true to life it was – did the butler really stay up, no matter what the time, until the lord and master decided to go to bed? He picked up the book and flicked through the pages to the several photographs. An airmail envelope, addressed to Monsieur S. Mercer, fell out. He opened it. Inside was a printed form from Credit Sempach, Geneva, which had been filled in advising that five thousand Swiss francs had been withdrawn from account xxxxxxx and paid into the account of Monsieur McCleary.

He stared into space. Had Faber fooled everyone?

When he returned to the sitting room Susan was on her

own. She stood, said she'd get the drinks, and left. She returned with a glass in each hand, passed one to him, and sat.

Thorne entered. 'So where's mine?'

'I thought you were having coffee.'

'Then you thought wrongly.'

'A case of great minds not thinking alike?'

He left, walking awkwardly.

Alvarez was surprised by the nature of their very brief conversation; it suggested they had recently had sharp words, if not a row.

'Your health,' she said, as she raised her glass.

'And yours, señora.'

'I seem to remember asking you to call me Susan.'

'I am sorry.'

'Keeping everything official?'

Not by choice. 'It helps.'

'Helps what?'

'To keep it official.'

She laughed.

Something he still couldn't determine – perhaps only a bad poet could – was why one woman would leave a man uninterested where another – however illogically – captured his full attention. He recognized that marriage created bars of steel and yet his traitorous mind insisted on wondering . . . 'When I was last here, you started to say something, but did not finish. What was it you did not say?'

'Obviously, it was nothing.' She smiled.

Mariano Figaredo had written in his book on the art of seduction that a woman with a sense of humour was a prime subject because she found sex so absurdly amusing. 'It was after I told you Señor Mercer had died in the crash; I gained the impression you thought that what you were about to say might have sounded unfeeling in the circumstances. It concerned what happened that last time he left here.'

'Now I remember . . . Why do you need to know? The poor man's dead.'

'I'm afraid it was not an accident.'

'What do you mean?'

'The car had been sabotaged.'

'But . . . My God, you're not saying . . .'

'It was murder.'

Thorne returned, glass in hand. He came to a stop and stared at his wife. 'Has something happened? You look as if you've seen a troop of ghosts.'

'It . . . it wasn't an accident.'

'What wasn't?'

'Steve's crash.'

'He deliberately drove off the edge?'

'It was murder,' Alvarez said quietly.

'Jesus!' Thorne sat.

'As you'll understand, I now have to conduct an investigation.'

'It doesn't seem possible.'

'It seldom does.'

'But who in the hell could possibly want to kill him?'

'That is what I have to find out. I'm hoping you'll be able to help me.'

'You surely don't think we know anything about it?'

'You may, señor, without realizing that fact.' He turned to Susan. 'What was it you didn't wish to tell me?'

'Steve had been drinking heavily before he drove off.'

He was disappointed. That was not news.

'I didn't like to say because it would have sounded as if I thought he deserved what happened.'

'I quite understand.' He drank. 'Clearly, someone hated or feared Señor Mercer. It's possible that when you've been here, either of you has heard or seen something which might help me determine who that someone could be.'

They looked at each other. Thorne said, 'It goes against the grain.'

'What does?'

'Mentioning something which seems to be accusing someone when they're most likely totally innocent.'

'What I am asking is if you can describe anything that might help me. If you can and it does, you will be accusing no one. It is I who will do that if there is reason to do so.'

'Suppose we do mention something, a name . . . Will people learn about us?'

'I can promise you no one will know.'

Thorne picked up his glass, drained it. 'I'm going to have the other half. Will you join me, Inspector?'

'Perhaps just a small one.' Alvarez passed his glass. He hoped his polite English hypocrisy would not result in little more than a mouthful.

'You are drinking what?'

'*Coñac*, with just ice, please.'

'Sue?' Thorne asked.

'I don't want any more.'

Thorne left the room. Alvarez asked Susan if she had seen any more of the island since they'd last spoken about it; she had not and still could not persuade her husband to drive along the coast to the newly restored *talyot*. Did Alvarez know all about *talyots*? He had to admit he knew very little. But, he hastily added, no one, not even the experts, could speak definitively about them.

Thorne returned, handed Alvarez a glass, and sat. 'What you're really asking us is, surely, was Steve at odds with anyone?'

'That is one of the questions I should like answered.'

'Well, there was trouble because of George . . .'

'No,' Susan said.

'Señora,' Alvarez said, 'I'm afraid I have to know.'

'But it's all becoming so . . . so nasty.'

'I am afraid a murder is always nasty.'

There was a silence, which Alvarez ended. 'Who is George?'

'George Varley. I don't suppose you know him.'

'I have met him if he is the friend of Señor Dale?'

'A friend some of the time.'

'It's only rumour,' she said.

'You're forgetting I was working here when they turned up.'

'Señor Varley and Señor Dale were here?' Alvarez asked.

'George was here one day and Terry the next. And there was one hell of a row between Steve and Terry. The windows were open, so unintentionally I had a listening grandstand.'

'What was the row about?'

'That's not obvious?'

'Señor Dale was annoyed Señor Varley had been here?'

'Jealously furious . . . But I'm certain Terry would never have messed around with the car. He just isn't up to harming anyone physically . . . You won't tell him what I've said to you?'

'I have already promised that.'

'I'm not questioning your word, Inspector; it's just me being worried about the people learning I've . . . well, not to put too fine a point on it, sneaked. We don't find it as easy to denounce someone as seems to be the case here.'

'Each country has its own customs. When did this row occur?'

'Maybe a week ago.'

'Last Monday?'

'Could be.'

'You can't be certain?'

Thorne was briefly silent. 'It was either Monday or Tuesday. Sorry, but I can't be any more definite than that.'

'Is there anyone else you should mention?'

'I . . . I suppose I ought to tell you about Fred Osborn as well.'

'Why bring him into it?' she demanded. 'Just because he snubbed you.'

'Don't be so bloody ridiculous.'

She momentarily looked alarmed. Fearful that later Thorne would vent his anger on her? Alvarez wondered. 'What does snubbed mean?'

'That social distinction is alive and flourishing.'

'I fear I still do not understand.'

'Equality is as much of a mirage as ever. It's just the boundary lines of inequality that have changed. Money is now the god of social distinction; background and manners are irrelevant. Terry Osborn still sees merit in claiming descent from the third son of a lady who tutored King Charles and was granted a title for the quality of her education. He expects to be treated with respect and objects to my lack of it.'

'That is interesting, señor, but why have you mentioned Señor Osborn?'

'He also had a row with Steve.'

'When was that?'

'A few days after the Dale incident.'

'What was the row about?'

'I have no idea. I was too far away to hear words, only the shouting.'

'Señor Mercer seems to have had difficult relations with people.'

'Yet he was always very friendly to us.'

Alvarez thought for a moment, then said, 'Thank you for your help.' He stood.

'Hang on. What do we do with Steve's possessions? Like I said, the boss wants us to drop them at the office, as is usual when a client snuffs it, but maybe you'll say differently?'

'For the moment, I should prefer them to stay where they are.'

'I'll tell the office.'

Alvarez said goodbye. Susan's smile was warm. Warmer than he might have expected? Dolores would claim that he had the imagination of a teenager.

Alvarez phoned Palma just after ten o'clock on Tuesday.

'Another emergency?' the secretary asked.

Poor jokes should be quickly buried.

'Yes?' said Salas.

'Yesterday evening, señor, I spoke to Señor and Señora Thorne and—'

'Yet again, you mention names without any explanation as to who they are.'

'They work for the agency which handles the letting of Villa Bellavista.'

'Where?

'That is the villa Señor Mercer was renting.'

'Then why not say so?'

'Señor, when in the past I have reminded you—'

'You do not remind me of something of which I am fully conversant. My question was one more attempt to provoke you into presenting a responsible report. You will restart, explaining carefully who is who and what is what.'

'Yesterday afternoon, I decided to go to Bellavista – that is the villa which was rented by Señor Mercer – to speak to Señor and Señora Thorne. They are married to each other.'

'You are trying to be a humorist?'

'No, señor.'

'Your intention is insolently to mock me?'

'Of course not.'

'Then you consider me incapable of recognizing a Señora Thorne is married to a Señor Thorne?'

'You have often advised me against assumptions, however obvious they seem to be. She could be a sister-in-law if the señor had a brother. Or even a cousin. That is, married to a cousin on the husband's side. Then there is the possibility, however faint, that two people of the same name, but unconnected by blood, meet and enjoy each other's company. The chances of that happening obviously have to be greater when a common name rather than an unusual one is concerned. How common is the name Thorne? One needs an Englishman's opinion on that . . .'

'Just tell me what happened with as little comment as possible.'

'While at the house, I asked to see what possessions Señor Mercer had left. Among these, I found a letter addressed to Mercer from Credit Sempach advising the transfer of five thousand Swiss francs to the account of McCleary. It is difficult to accept such a letter would be in the hands of anyone other than the person to whom the envelope was addressed. Unless, of course, by chance . . .'

'You will ignore any other possibility.'

'So it seems probable, if not certain, that Faber had more than one foreign account. A reasoned assumption would be that the stolen money was deposited in a bank which received deposits without any genuine investigation into their source and he had an account in another bank, fed from the first, which was accepted as totally reliable by the international authorities so that this account would never arouse any interest – that is, interest of a financial nature . . .'

'Remain within the facts.'

'Yes, señor.'

'Does it occur to you that all this can only make sense if Mercer was Faber?'

'Yes, señor.'

'Extraordinary! You claim you have identified Faber and send the English police a photograph of Mercer. They reply he is not Faber. Yet now you build assumptions on the assumption that he was.'

'The English could have made a mistake. I think we should ask them to check.'

'You expect me to do that, on the word of an inspector who made a previous ridiculous, boastful claim—'

'I made no such boast, señor. It was you said that—'

'And I am now saying I have no intention of making the Cuerpo any more of a laughing stock than it already is because of your incompetence.' Salas slammed down the receiver.

It was, Alvarez reluctantly acknowledged, unlikely the English police would have made so gross a visual mistake, but it was not impossible. And who was McCleary? Why had the letter been in Mercer's possession? And where had the five thousand Swiss francs sprung from?

Sixteen

Alvarez parked in front of Ca'n Trestar, climbed out of his car. The day sparkled with sunshine, yet for him the mountains so close to the house remained grimly threatening. Rock fractured, faces collapsed, thousand of tonnes engulfed all. He could be standing there one moment alive and well, the next pinned down by rocks which slowly and agonizingly squeezed all life out of him . . .

'I was wondering when next we would have the pleasure of your company, Inspector.'

He swung round to face Varley.

'Perhaps you have come to tell us the truth of the girl with ginger hair?'

Alvarez's dislike of the other increased. 'Is Señor Dale here?'

'In the pool, trying to persuade himself he can swim. Presumably, you want to speak to him?'

'Yes.'

'It will be a kindness to me as well as him if you remember he has a nervous disposition. Will you come on through?'

Dale sat on one of the lower steps of the pool, the water up to his chest.

'As you will observe, Terry,' Varley said, 'we again have the pleasure of the inspector's presence. He wishes to have a chat with you. About cabbages and kings? Time will answer.'

Dale muttered a good afternoon.

'I will leave you to yourselves,' Varley said. 'A man should always have the politeness to absent himself when he is about to be discussed.'

'Where are you going?' Dale asked nervously.

'To buy an English paper.'

'Can't you wait?'

'And find all choice eliminated? Even no news is preferable to *Sun* news.' He spoke to Alvarez. 'Terry can be rather forgetful, so have no hesitation in reminding him you would like a drink. And as you may well have left by the time I return, goodbye and may your day be fruitful.'

And may yours be barren, Alvarez silently replied.

As Varley returned inside, Dale launched himself off the steps in a flurry of water, swam a clumsy breaststroke until level with Alvarez, then put his feet down. 'What is it now?'

'Would it not be easier for both of us if you got out of the pool?'

Dale ploughed back through the water to the steps and climbed them. He walked past Alvarez, sat on one of the folding wood-and-canvas chairs in the shade of the small patio.

It seemed Varley's words regarding a drink had been forgotten or were being ignored, Alvarez gloomily decided as he settled on a second chair.

'George keeps saying . . .' Dale stopped.

'Yes, señor?'

'There never was a woman with ginger hair. Was it a subterfuge?'

'You can hardly expect me to admit there was no such person.'

'You're as good as admitting it was just a story.'

'I don't think I'm admitting anything.'

'Why are you here again?'

'To learn if you can help me. You will have heard about the unfortunate death of Señor Mercer?'

'Of course I have. But what's that to do with me?'

'It was not an accident. The car had been sabotaged.'

'My God!'

'So you'll understand I have to find out who was responsible.'

'But you can't think . . .'

'Señor, I am talking to you because anyone who knew the señor may be able to help me.'

'I didn't know him. I hardly ever spoke to him.'

'Yet you visited his house a week ago and had a heated argument with him.'

'No.'

'I have been told that is what happened.'

'It's a lie.'

'Why should someone lie about such a thing?'

'How could I know? People can be bastards.'

'Señor, I seek only the truth and when I know it and am certain it is of no importance, it will be forgotten.'

'There wasn't a row.'

'Yet you did visit Señor Mercer's house.'

There was a long pause before Dale finally muttered, 'Yes.' Then he added, speaking loudly, 'It was only for a very short time.'

'Time enough to have a heated row.'

'I keep telling you, there wasn't one.'

'Why did you go to Señor Mercer's house if normally you seldom spoke to him?'

'There was something I wanted to say.'

'What?'

'I've forgotten.'

'You worked for many years for agricultural engineers, didn't you?'

'Why do you want to know?'

'Your job was in accounts, yet over the years you will have learned a considerable amount about machinery. Would you say there are basic similarities between hydraulic systems in agricultural machinery and cars?'

'How was the car sabotaged?'

'A brake line was damaged in such a way that, under heavy braking, it would fracture and the brakes on one side of the car would become inoperative.'

'You're trying to say I . . . that I . . . Christ! Why should I want to kill him?'

'Perhaps because Señor Varley had become very friendly with him.'

'That's crazy.'

'Señor, when someone lies, it is because he wishes to hide something. What are you hiding if not the fact that you sabotaged Señor Mercer's car?'

'I'm not hiding anything. I never touched his car.'

Alvarez watched a dragonfly perform gymnastics above the pool, its wings glistening as it turned. 'You live in Arlington Cross?'

'Yes.'

'Do you remember my asking you if that was near Eddington?'

'No.'

'You answered it was not. I found the distance was about six miles. Since most people in a world of cars would call that quite close, I presumed you lied for a certain reason. I learned that that was wrong. So now I wonder if your lie indicated you were panicking because you were afraid that to answer correctly might, however illogical, expose something you were desperate to hide. Am I correct?'

'I don't know what you're talking about.'

'Are you married?'

'I've told you, I'm not.'

'What is your home address?'

'Why do you want to know?'

'I will ask someone in England to check you are telling me the truth.'

Dale's expression betrayed his fear.

'Señor, let me explain once again that if what you tell me has no bearing on the murder of Señor Mercer, what you say will be forgotten.'

'I . . .' Dale gestured with his hands. He stood, walked across to the edge of the pool and stared down at the water.

Alvarez was silent. Silence could unnerve far more than words.

Dale returned and sat, fidgeted with arm of the chair. 'I . . . I am married.' The words seemed to be dragged out of him.

'Your wife is at your home in England?'

'She's in the Bahamas . . .' He stopped, paused, then spoke rapidly, trying to excuse as he confessed.

Life had not been kind to him. His father had held to the strictest principles, moral and social; his mother had had a weak character. Money had been sufficient, but never plentiful – his father would never cut corners and believed rules to be sacrosanct, and such a man would never be employed in a senior job. At great financial sacrifice his parents had sent him to a third-rate public school and there his friendship with a fellow pupil, Donald, had resolved his sexual preferences.

He had gone from school to a technical college which had become a university. He had gained a two-one and, thanks to a family friend, a good job. Although moral standards had changed, he could not escape moral guilt, largely fuelled by the certainty of how his father would respond if he ever learned the truth. Guilt had caused him to try to bury his preferred lifestyle and lead a normal social life. He had met Veronica and after a few months had proposed to her; she had accepted. His father had expressed his pleasure by remarking Veronica was no beauty, but she would maintain a Christian home; his mother had nervously asked him if he was sure he should marry Veronica, making it clear that she had suspected his homosexuality for a long time.

Marriage taught him he should have heeded his mother's unspoken warning; his father had taught him that one must face the consequences of one's actions.

Veronica's uncle had become rich through inventing kitchen utensils that nobody needed but everyone wanted. He had died suddenly and, to her surprise, she had learned she was his heir. She'd always had an extravagant nature, but Dale's salary had restricted her excesses; now there was no such limitation. They had moved into a much larger, prestigious house, had luxury holidays, ate at expensive restaurants without a thought as to the cost, and gained a circle of friends who respected money as much as she did.

By chance he discovered she was having an affair. He considered divorcing her, but wealth was a potent drug. If he was content to suffer her infidelities, he could continue to enjoy the life she provided; if not, he would once more have to live on what he earned. So when she told him she needed a break and was off to the Bahamas with Mary (Ian or Sam? Or someone he had not yet learned about?), he had wished her a happy holiday. He had come to Mallorca and met George Varley. If Veronica ever learned about this, she would, being totally selfish, cut him out of her life.

'Thank you for telling me,' Alvarez said.

'It makes me seem . . .'

'Like any other human, señor.' He paused for a moment, then said, 'You have explained one lie. Will you now explain another? What was the subject of the fierce row you had with Señor Mercer?'

'It wasn't fierce.'

'You admit there was this row?'

'I . . . Yes.'

'What was it about?'

'I told him not to encourage George.'

'You objected very strongly?'

'I may have shouted once or twice.'

'And threatened?'

'No.'

'Are you certain?'

'Do I look the kind of person to offer violence?'

'A threat can be made without the intention to carry it out.'

'I didn't threaten him.'

'What was Señor Mercer's response to what you said?'

'He laughed. Hadn't I learned that a bee always visited a pansy with the most pollen.'

'That angered you?'

'It made me . . . despise myself a little more.'

The world was a cruel place.

Alvarez stared through the unshuttered window, tried and failed to find a valid reason for not phoning Salas. He dialled.

'Yes?

'Señor, I have questioned Dale. The reason for his lie about the distance of his house from Eddington is that he is married.'

'You suggest it is normal to lie when one is married?'

'And necessary.'

'A ridiculous comment.'

'He lied for fear that if he said he lived quite close to Faber, I would have reason to talk to his wife when she returned and she would learn about his life here. She is very wealthy and has gone to the Bahamas with a lover.

Because of that, Dale decided he might as well find some pleasure and—'

'There is no need to go any further.'

'It is necessary to explain.'

'But not necessary to hear such explanation.'

'Then you may not understand what I say.'

'Why should you think that to be unusual?'

'He lied about being married and exactly where he lived for fear his wife would learn he was here with Varley. So the assumption that if he lied over a small matter he was likely to lie over a major one does not hold.'

'As an intelligent officer would have known.'

'He admits to having a row with Mercer, but calls it loud, not fierce; it was occasioned by Señor Varley having been encouraged by Mercer to visit him . . .'

'You will explain no further.'

'Clearly, the fact he worked for an agricultural engineering firm means he must have learned much practical information about hydraulic lines, even if he was in the office – he probably had friends on the floor and they talked about their work. It's extraordinary how one can pick up the whole from small parts – rather like a jigsaw puzzle.'

'Are you now about to introduce crossword puzzles?'

'He had motive and method.'

'If I can disentangle the verbiage, you mark him as your prime suspect?'

'He appears to be. And yet I find it very difficult to believe him capable of planning and executing murder.'

'Your reluctance makes it more likely.'

'Señor, I have another witness to question, one who also had an argument with Señor Mercer.'

'Why have you not already questioned him?'

'It's a question of time.'

'A question to which you pay little heed. Have you

pursued the source of the money paid into McCleary's account in Switzerland?'

'Not yet, señor.'

'No doubt you fail to understand the importance of doing so.'

'Far from it.'

'Have you asked the bank for details?'

'It's a Swiss bank.'

'You have at least understood that?'

'Swiss banks won't divulge details of accounts unless it can be proved the money in them is illegal.'

'You will not, of course, have yet examined Mercer's possessions, looking for such proof.'

'I have, very thoroughly, but there were no personal papers of any description and that's odd; even odder was the lack of a single credit or cash card. It makes me wonder . . .'

'Well?

'If Mercer's identity was thrice false. That would explain the lack of credit cards since, to obtain one, it's necessary to prove identity and financial standing. Perhaps he was Faber in England, McCleary in Geneva and Mercer here. But why the treble impersonations? Wouldn't it have been far simpler to leave England with one name, bank in Geneva and live here with another?'

'You continue with the absurd claim that Mercer was Faber when it has been proved on unimpeachable evidence that he was not.'

'People make mistakes.'

'Who would know better than you?'

'If England tell us that Mercer's passport was a forgery, this could just be enough to persuade Credit Sempach to tell us what they can about the account there.'

'This is something which should have been done a long time ago. However, I will personally make the request in order that it is understood.' He rang off.

Alvarez replaced the receiver, settled back in the chair. A gecko scuttled up the wall to the window, wriggled its way outside. Salas lacked the ability to understand one did not have to be a fool to do things incorrectly.

He lit a cigarette. His mind wandered to more personal matters. If he were to make progress, he must ask Raquel out to a meal to prove his generosity and his emotional regard for her, whether she was rich or poor. What better time to issue the invitation than now, when there was no fear of Dolores's overhearing him?

Margarita asked him to wait because Doña Rexach was out in the garden, talking to Rafael. He mused on the future. He would suggest Margarita remain at Sa Echona, but that Rafael be replaced. Not only was Rafael clearly stubborn and unimaginative, on the one occasion they had spoken professionally, Rafael had argued about the best quarter of the moon during which to prune olive trees.

'Enrique, how nice to hear from you,' Raquel said. 'Are you at home?'

'At the post, working myself to death.'

'If ever I've met a man with enough sense not to do that, it's you.'

He was uncertain whether or not that was a compliment. 'I wondered if you were free tomorrow evening to have dinner?'

'Let me check my appointments' book. I have a feeling something is happening.'

She would be meeting a high-born, handsome man, clever, witty, amusing. How could he hope to compete? He was a fool . . .

'I was right, I am supposed to be meeting someone. But I could cancel if you insist?'

'I insist.'

'How pleasant to meet a man who knows how a man should behave.'

'When shall I pick you up?'

'Suppose you arrive here at eight. That will allow time to have a drink.'

He said goodbye. As he replaced the receiver, he wondered with a sense of scornful triumph who was to be denied her company this time? Clearly, someone who might have all the social graces but was not a real man.

Seventeen

As Alvarez drove into Urbanización Bernejo and parked, three young women wearing bikinis, carrying towels, walked past him on their way to the beach. In the past, he might have admired their sleek forms and perhaps even fantasized a little, but recently he had learned more sense. As the old Mallorquin saying reminded those who were prepared to listen, 'A woman's heart is truth, her beauty, a lie.' He continued to watch the three until they went out of sight. The middle one vaguely reminded him of Susan, perhaps because of the neatness of her bottom. He realized the engine was still running and switched it off.

He left the car, walked through the garden of pebbles – the solitary hibiscus looked ready to die – and knocked on the front door of Ca'n Federico. It was opened by Osborn.

'Good morning, señor. I should like to have a word with you. May I enter?'

Osborn said nothing, moved back. He stepped into the tiny hall. 'Is Señor Pollard here?'

'No.'

After a moment, Alvarez said, 'Perhaps we might sit somewhere?'

Osborn turned, went through the sitting room to outside. Chairs had been set as on Alvarez's previous visit, this time in the sun.

'Would you mind if I move into the shade, señor?' Alvarez asked.

'Do what you want. Everyone else does.'

He lifted a patio chair into the shade and sat.

'I suppose you'd like a drink?'

'Thank you.'

'What?'

'*Coñac* with just ice, please.'

Osborn returned into the bungalow.

Whatever was so disturbing the other was, Alvarez judged, primarily not likely to be fear of the police or he would have tried to be pleasant, not sullenly rude.

Osborn returned with a glass in each hand, passed one to Alvarez, sat, drank quickly.

'Señor, you will know Señor Mercer died in a car crash?'

'Yes.'

'Have you also heard his car had been sabotaged, which was why it crashed?'

'Bloody hell!' He drank even more quickly, almost emptying the glass.

'I'm here to learn if you can tell me anything which might help me identify the murderer.'

'How can I when I hardly knew the man. Look, can't we do this some other time?'

'I'm afraid not.'

'I'm . . . I'm very upset.'

'I am sorry to hear that.'

'You trust someone and he turns round and kicks you in the goolies. He was just out for what he could get; his friendship was totally bloody false.'

'You are referring to Señor Pollard?'

'Said he must buy some new clothes to wear because all his were looking shabby. I drew money on my card and gave it to him.'

'And he's not returned?'

Osborn shook his head.

Since it was likely Pollard frequently worked this scam,

details should be circulated to all Cuerpo posts. The second time he had come to such a decision. 'How much did you give him?'

'Two hundred euros. It was more than I could really afford, but . . .' He became miserably silent.

Pollard could not have gained any indication that Osborn had become a wealthy man through theft or he would have asked for very much more. An indication of Osborn's innocence or proof of very tight lips? 'Señor, I will ask you again: how well did you know Señor Mercer?'

'I did not kill him.'

'That is not what I asked.'

'You think I could have.'

'I have to consider all possibilities. And the more often you avoid answering my questions, the more I consider that a possibility may well be a probability.'

'He wasn't a friend.'

'But you met?'

'Occasionally.'

'You were in his house a few days before he died.'

'No.'

'There are witnesses who say you were and that you had a row with him.'

'I didn't kill him. Why won't you believe me? I couldn't kill anyone.'

'If you tell me the truth, I am more likely to believe you.'

'I'm too upset.'

'To tell the truth?'

Osborn raised his glass and drained it. He abruptly stood and went indoors, returned with a refilled glass, sat down. 'Tom . . .' He paused. 'Tom said he was going down to the front after supper to watch the people: the woman imitating a statue he couldn't make laugh, the hucksters, the ancients. He said it was like seeing humanity in all its shapes and sizes. I stayed here because that sort of thing bores me. He didn't return until the early morning, said he'd been drinking at the bars with a chap he'd known back in England. A couple of days later, Frank enjoyed telling me Tom seemed to be very friendly with Steve Mercer. I asked Tom if that was true. He laughed and said Steve was far too superior and complicated to be a friend of anyone. They'd met, chatted, cursed the government back home, and parted.

'Two days later I decided not to go with him when he said he wanted a walk. Then I found I hadn't any cigarettes and drove down to one of the tobacconists. There's a bar next to it and I saw them there.'

'What happened?'

'I drove off. I decided I had to speak to Steve and ask him not to spoil my friendship with Tom.'

'You went to Villa Bellavista?'

After a moment Osborn nodded.

'How did Señor Mercer respond to what you said?'

'He laughed. He enjoyed seeing me hurt.'

'So there was a row?'

'I said things I'd rather not have done because it made me look so weak and small.'

'Did you threaten him?'

'No . . . Not really.'

'What does that mean?'

'I told him that if he didn't stop encouraging Tom, I'd make him stop.'

'How were you going to do that?'

'It was just talk.'

'Then it was only later it occurred to you to sabotage his car?'

'For God's sake, I didn't do it. Why won't you understand?'

'You had reason to hate Mercer.'

'There are a lot of people I hate, but I don't try to kill them.'

'You run a car?'

'A small one.'

'So you'll know where the brake lines run.'

'You . . . You're accusing me.'

'No. Just understanding the facts.'

'I've told you the truth.'

Alvarez stood. 'I imagine you have no plans to leave the island in the near future?'

Osborn's voice rose. 'It doesn't matter what I say, you think I killed him. Oh, God, how do I make you realize I didn't?'

'If you did not, the facts will do that.'

Alvarez was glad to drive out of the *urbanización*. The small, tightly bunched bungalows, covering land which had once been open and green, depressed him; Osborn's evidence depressed him; the certainty that there were many others whose lives were equally troubled, depressed him. He needed a drink.

Port Llueso had a maze of one-way roads and because his thoughts were elsewhere, he found himself in a dead end. He swore, reversed. Just beyond the port on the Llueso road, he passed two fields in which dozens of boats were stored to await their owners' appearance – could money be wasted more efficiently than by buying a boat and paying to have it aground?

In the dining room at home, Jaime sat at the table and contemplated the bottle in front of himself. Alvarez brought a glass out of the sideboard, poured himself a drink.

'I've had one hell of a morning,' Jaime said lugubriously.

'Mine's not been all smiles.'

Dolores stepped through the bead curtain. 'Truly, I am fortunate to lead so carefree a life.'

They studied the table.

'Even so, it is not perfect. The kitchen is a furnace because my husband has not mended the fan – was it two or three months ago he promised to do it the next day? But then, he is a very busy man and I do not like to bother him.'

'If only,' Jaime muttered.

'What did you say?' she snapped.

'I will mend the fan as soon as possible.'

'Would it interest you both to know what kind of a day I have been having?'

They did not answer.

'I prepared the meal as far as possible before the actual cooking. I dusted the downstairs shutters. Some time ago, my husband promised to do that, but his memory is not always reliable. Then I tidied the rooms. I will not mention the mess in Enrique's room since all men are incurably untidy. Afterwards, there was the shopping. There are shops close by, but I go to ones further away because they have the food I know my men prefer. A dutiful wife always considers the men before herself. The bags of shopping were heavy, but that's of no account. Of course, my morning's work is as nothing compared to the burden you two have endured. So do not feel sorry for me.' She returned to the kitchen.

'Women are always making a fuss about nothing,' Jaime muttered.

'Have you remembered?' Dolores called out.

They looked at each other, wondering who was about to be proved at fault.

'Will they need passports or will their ID cards be enough?'

Alvarez relaxed; this was not his problem. He poured himself another drink.

'Well?'

'I tried to phone,' Jaime said, 'but every time the line was engaged.'

She stepped into the room. 'Then you must keep on trying now until the line is free.'

'It's no good.'

'Why not?'

'It's lunch time.'

'A man can always find reason for not doing something.' She returned into the kitchen.

Jaime looked at the bead curtain, decided she was too busy to reappear quickly, refilled his glass.

'What's the problem over passports?' Alvarez asked.

'The school's organizing a voyage of studies to Carcassonne and Isabel and Juan are going on it.'

'Surely ID cards are enough?'

'How would I know? And come to that, you should.'

'You'll likely find no one does.' He drank. The mention of passports reminded him Salas needed Mercer's in order to send it back to England. It was lucky Jaime had failed to carry out what he had been asked to do. One man's incompetence could be another's saviour.

Eighteen

Susan opened the front door.

'My apologies yet again,' Alvarez said, 'but this time I shall not be bothering you for long. I have to collect something from Señor Mercer's possessions and when I have done that, I will leave you in peace.'

'The presumption being, that is what I would wish?'

It was an odd question. She presented a proselytizing figure to a man who had accepted that female beauty was a false guide. Her blouse was curvaceous, her skirt barely adequate.

'Are you going to remain standing there?'

He stepped inside and as she shut the door, she brushed against him. How old was the man who did not wonder which part of a woman had made brief contact with him?

'You're very quiet,' she said.

'I've a lot to think about.'

'Pleasant thoughts, I trust?'

Dangerous thoughts. 'If it's all right, I'll go up to the bedroom.'

'On your own?'

She seemed ignorant of, or indifferent to, the impression her words might provoke in the mind of a salacious man. 'I know the way, thanks.'

'Then carry on your solitary way.'

He crossed to the stairs and climbed them, more actively than if she had not been watching; on his arrival at the top, he was short of breath. Mercer's room was untouched. He picked up the passport and the note from Credit Sempach, returned downstairs. She stood by the open doorway and the bright sunshine beyond turned her dress virtually transparent; she was not wearing a petticoat.

'Have you got what you wanted?' she asked.

'Yes, thank you.'

'Everything you wanted? You were very quick. Are you always so easily satisfied?'

'I hope so.'

'How very unambitious. Now you can come and talk to me while we have a drink.'

'I'm afraid I must leave . . .'

'Work is more interesting than my company?'

'On the contrary, but I have to earn a living.'

'Your earning will have to wait. I've poured a brandy and I don't like that. I hate waste.'

'Perhaps if I am not too long.'

'How long is too long?'

'The time it takes for my superior chief to wonder where I am and what I am doing.'

'If he bothers you, I'll tell him you were watching my every movement.'

It was easy to imagine Salas's reaction to that.

'Let's go through.'

He did not want to appear rude so objected no further.

There were two glasses on a marble working surface in the kitchen and she picked them up, handed him one. 'We'll sit by the pool. It's so much more cheerful than this gloomy place.'

Gloomy? he thought, as he followed her. But then he liked rock walls because they made the building part of the land.

By the side of the pool, chairs had again been set around the table, which supported a sun umbrella. They sat.

'You always prefer shade to sun?' she said.

'Yes, I do.'

'For shady reasons?'

'Because I burn rather easily.'

'You're being very serious. Are you on your guard?'

Only against himself.

'I don't burn easily, so I enjoy as much sun as possible. If you weren't here, I'd strip off and sunbathe starkers.' She turned and looked at him. 'Would that embarrass you?'

'If I weren't here, how could I be embarrassed?'

'That's being pedantic. Come on, confess.'

'I'd be surprised.'

'You don't like surprises?'

Could she not realize her playful words might lead a man to expressing a very vocal desire to be surprised? From his arrival, her manner had been unusual. Was she emotionally upset? Increased discord between spouses?

'You've become silent again.'

'I apologize.'

'A centimo for your thoughts.'

'They cost more than that.'

'How much more?'

'Impossible to judge.'

'Then I'll have to guess your thoughts. Would you like to know what my guess is?'

'Not really.'

'What a boring answer.'

'I imagine I am a boring person.'

'You imagination needs . . . I was going to say stimulating, but perhaps the problem is, it is too active already?' She smiled.

Her smile could lead a man into hell. 'I am about to become even more boring because I have to ask some questions.'

'And if I refuse to answer them?'

'Perhaps I will arrest you for obstructing justice.'

'Handcuffs and humiliation?'

'Your husband told me he was in the garden when Señor Dale and Señor Mercer had an argument. I forgot to ask if you also were there, although I believe you were. Is that so?'

'Correct, Inspector Enrique.'

'Your husband . . .'

'Call him Dick. It sounds so much less constricting.'

'He described it as one hell of a row. Yet it has also been said to me that it was a loud, but not an angry argument. What would you say?'

'Opinions differ.'

'What would yours be?'

'It was certainly loud.'

'And fierce?'

'Hard to judge when I was upstairs, tidying and dusting.'

'You must have gained an impression.'

'Are you telling or asking?'

'I'm asking you to help.'

'Which I'm doing all I can so that you don't curb my opposition with handcuffs. The walls of this place are thick and absorb sound. I was aware they were arguing loudly, but couldn't say how angrily. Surely, Dick's opinion is good enough?'

'It helps to have an opinion corroborated.'

'Then I'll corroborate it.'

'You've just said you can't.'

'I'm only trying to help.'

'It's hardly helping when you say something that's obviously untrue.'

'If it's that obvious, it won't bother you, since you'll know it is untrue.'

'You are not being helpful.'

'I was warned against ever helping a man in case he took advantage of my easy nature.'

'I have no intention of taking advantage of you.'

'Ever boring!'

'Did Señor Mercer always garage his car?'

'He seldom bothered because the angle of approach into the garage is tricky on account of the stone wall on the right.'

'So the car would often be left standing outside the garage?'

'Most times.'

'All night?'

'Why do you think I can answer that?'

'I am not suggesting . . .' He stopped.

'What are you not suggesting, Inspector Enrique?'

'I wondered if you often arrived in the morning and found the car outside?'

'If he seldom garaged it, would you not expect that?'

'Did you ever see anyone showing interest in his car?'

'What kind of interest?'

'An unusual one.'

'It's difficult to imagine what would be unusual when men get so excited over cars. Do you see them as sex symbols?'

'Merely as something to get me from A to B.'

'How boringly practical!'

'Señora—'

'How many times do I have to remind you I'm Susan? When you call me señora, I'm afraid you're all official because you're about to arrest me. Would you visit me in my cell, dry my tears, put your arms around me and comfort me?'

'Please be sensible.'

'You want a woman to be down-to-earth? Rather uncomfortable.'

Did she ever think before she spoke? 'Did you see anyone hanging around the car when it was outside?'

'No. How much longer are you going to abuse me?'

'I have done nothing of the sort.'

'You keep asking me questions.'

'I don't think I have any more.'

'Then we can relax, have another drink, and talk about the birds and the bees.'

'I am afraid I must leave.' He stood.

' "Afraid" is just about the right word.'

Her tone had suddenly become hard. Like all women, she became annoyed the moment her wishes were not met.

He sat at his desk, lifted the receiver and dialled Palma. Salas's secretary did not ask him what the emergency was.

'Yes?' said Salas.

'Señor, I have just returned from Villa Bellavista. That is the house Señor Mercer was renting. Señor Mercer died in a serious—'

'If you offer someone coffee, do you carefully explain it is hot?'

Alvarez stared at the far wall and wondered if the superior chief had already begun his evening drinking. 'I'm not quite certain what you mean, señor.'

'I object to having my valuable time wasted by an inspector who thinks it necessary to underline the obvious.'

'But previously you have criticized me for not doing so. I am becoming confused. Do you want me to identify the persons I'm talking about, señor, or do you not? I ask because when I didn't, you did, and now I do, you don't.'

'Talking to you, Alvarez, encompasses the art of incomprehension. Am I ever going to learn the reason for this call?'

'To inform you that I have Señor Mercer's passport and

the letter from Credit Sempach. Shall I read out the details of the passport so that you can query them with England?'

'Yes.'

Alvarez began to speak, was immediately checked.

'My secretary will note the details. Have you arranged for the bank letter to reach me immediately?'

'Not yet, señor.'

'Why not?'

'I have only just returned to the office.'

'Small excuse for negligence.'

'But if I have only—'

'I want it here before I cease work this evening.'

'I don't think that's possible because . . .' He was talking to a dead phone.

Alvarez stepped into the kitchen.

'I was beginning to think you were not working today,' Dolores said.

'I'm not all that late.'

'By your standards, I suppose that is true.'

'I'll bet Salas doesn't start work dead on time every morning.'

She poured out a mug of hot chocolate. 'Madrileños are only good at telling others what to do.'

He sat at the table. 'Is there some coca?'

'You think there might not be?'

If she was in a bad mood, that was more than likely. He added two spoonfuls of sugar to the chocolate, stirred. Dolores brought half a *coca* out of one of the cupboards, used a knife to cut a slice which she put on a plate and passed this to him. He ate, drank, cleared his throat. 'Before I forget, I'll not be here for supper tomorrow.'

'Very well.'

'I hope you don't mind?'

'Why should I?'

'It might upset your arrangements.'

'I am used to that.'

'I hope you are not going to cook something special?'

'It will be a very ordinary meal.'

'You couldn't cook a very ordinary meal if you tried.'

'Is her cooking so much better than mine?'

He felt as if he had swallowed an iceberg. 'How do you mean?'

'Is Raquel's cooking better than my cooking?'

'I've no idea what hers is like, but I can be certain it can't match yours.'

'As my mother used to say, "When a man admits ignorance, he is ashamed of the truth."'

'Are you suggesting I've eaten at her place?'

'You have forgotten?'

'When am I supposed to have done that?'

'Saturday.'

'I was out with the young Englishwoman.'

'What did she serve? Caviar, smoked salmon, lobster, sole, fillet steak, partridge, *bombe surprise* and *baba au rhum*? She is incapable of understanding excess demonstrates a lack of taste.'

'I took her to the old fishermen's restaurant in the port because she'd never eaten local food. The hotel where she's staying only serves tourist food.'

'You think me blind and deaf?'

'I swear—'

'All too frequently.' She picked up a saucepan from the draining board and banged it down on the cooker to express her feelings. 'All the times you have chased a foreign woman, what has happened?'

'Since they're not like you imagine, nothing.'

'Does the truth forever pass you by? Now to try to make me believe your lie, you invent a foreign *puta*, half your age.'

'That's being ridiculous. Just because Raquel ate some ice cream in front of you—'

'It was chocolate.'

'Whatever it was. You—'

'Had you noted the joy with which she tormented us, your eyes might be able to see.'

'She was a kid and probably didn't realize you hadn't had any kind of sweets for ages.'

'You speak about something of which you know nothing.'

'But it all happened years ago; people change when they grow up. And since I wasn't at school with her, why should she want to try to hurt me?'

'Because she knows that if she hurts you, she will be hurting me.'

'If that's all she wants, she'd go for you direct.'

'When she knows I am too strong to be hurt by the likes of her?'

'Then she's not going to do as you keep suggesting, because she can be certain it'll be a complete waste of time.'

'You refuse to understand that she cannot hurt me face to face, but if she hurts someone I love, then she can succeed.'

'You're seeing something which just isn't so. I am having supper with the young English lady.'

'Do not strain your imagination any further.' She pulled up a chair and sat on the opposite side of the table. She spoke quietly, beseechingly. 'Enrique, please believe me when I tell you Raquel is a woman of infinite vindictiveness. She cannot forgive or forget; she will do anything, hurt anyone, to gain revenge. The sweeter she behaves, the more she is to be feared; the kinder she is, the more she wishes to injure.'

'Look at things logically . . .'

'You prefer not to understand? Then you must find out for yourself and I will suffer as you do. What is a woman's life but suffering?'

'I think you are totally wrong about her.'

'You have made that very clear.'

'I'm sorry if I've upset you, but—'

'Do not mock me.' Worried, frustrated, angered by the stupidity of men, she stood and marched through the bead curtain.

He drank the rest of the hot chocolate and ate the last of the slice of *coca*, certain that not even God moved in more mysterious ways than women.

Nineteen

Alvarez stared through the window of his office. A man had only to congratulate himself on his cleverness to be proved a fool. Why had he not continued to deny he was going out with a foreign woman so that Dolores would have been convinced he was? Now that she knew he was seeing Raquel, life at home was likely to be grim; she might even claim to be suffering from some female complaint and tell them they would have to get their own meals.

The phone rang. 'The superior chief will speak to you,' Salas's secretary said in lofty tones.

He waited.

'Where is the letter?' were Salas's opening words.

'What letter is that, señor?'

'Do I have to instruct you in every aspect of your case? The letter saying money has been paid into an account in the name of McCleary. Perhaps you have already forgotten that you informed me there was a letter amongst the dead man's property from a bank advising Mercer, under a pseudonym, that a sum of money had been paid into an account in the bank in Liechtenstein in the name of McCleary?'

'Geneva, señor.'

'What about Geneva?'

'Credit Sempach, which is the bank in question—'

'I am well aware of that.'

'It is not in Liechtenstein.'

'Where is it?'

'Geneva.'

'I am asking you where is the letter you said you would send to me immediately? It has not arrived here. Kindly answer the question I put and do not quibble over minor details.'

He had forgotten about the letter because of life's complications. 'I posted it at the first opportunity and it should have reached you this morning. Of course, one cannot rely on the post being as efficient as it should be . . .'

'You observed the regulations concerning the transmission of important documents?'

One more thing he had forgotten. It was frightening how one simple, harmless lie could lead into a thicket of thorny lies. If he claimed he had done as required – sent the letter by recorded delivery – Salas would ask for details and then complain to the post office; they would very soon make it clear no such letter had been sent . . . 'No, señor.'

'You ignored standing orders?'

'The post office was closed since they don't work the same long hours we have to and had I carried out your order to use recorded delivery, I would have had to wait until this morning. It seemed better to post normally last night since it had to reach you at the first possible moment.'

'Which it has failed to do.'

'I don't see how I can be blamed for that if it is the post office at fault.'

There was a short pause before Salas said, 'Neither have I had a report from you.'

'If you are referring to the Mercer case, señor, I have questioned several persons.'

'Have you learned anything of significance?'

'The situation at the moment is that I have obtained

several possible leads, but these have to be followed up before I can judge whether or not they are significant.'

'It would show some initiative if you had checked them rather than sitting in your office.'

'I was about to leave to do so when you rang.'

'Why has it taken you half the morning to get that far?'

'There is much other work which has to be done and it seemed to me better to wait to question everyone since the English are very slow risers.'

'We adapt our investigation to their sybaritic slackness?'

'As you will know, when one normally rises late—'

'I do not know, since I rise very early every day of the week.'

Which probably explained much. 'People can become very aggrieved if their routine is upset and then they don't co-operate as readily as they might.'

'A good interrogator does not need the willing co-operation of his subject. However, in your case you require all you can get. You will inform me as soon as you learn anything of significance.'

'Of course, señor. And if the passport proves to be the forgery I feel certain it is, I do think we ought to consider the possibility, however bizarre it might seem, that Faber and Mercer are the same person.'

Salas replaced the receiver.

Seniority clearly destroyed imagination. Alvarez found no difficulty in imagining that someone in England had, through ignorance or carelessness, incorrectly decided the dead man in the photograph was not Faber.

It was still a fraction too early safely to leave for his *merienda*, so he lit a cigarette. He wondered where to take Raquel for dinner the next evening. The two restaurants he most favoured were probably not a good idea because the clientele could be rough and the food was very Mallorquin. There were three or four where the food was reasonable and cosmopolitan, but they were frequented by foreigners and their prices excessive.

He went downstairs. The duty *cabo* asked him if he intended returning to work before it was time to stop. Most amusing.

The barman was clearly in a sullen mood. He hardly spoke and the size of the brandy Alvarez was served was hardly any larger than a member of the public would have been given. Trouble at home? Alvarez crossed to a window table and sat. Rosa, the other's wife, was reputed to have a temper as sharp as the thorns of her floral namesake.

He poured the remaining brandy into the coffee, lit a cigarette. Soon he must return to work – or at least to the office. Was he making any progress in the case? In truth, he had learned nothing to suggest who was responsible for sabotaging the car. Motive was often the signpost to the murderer, but although Osborne and Dale had motives, there was as yet no evidence to link either of them with the murder. They would have to be questioned again and each made aware he was under sharp suspicion. Guilt squeezed a man's conscience.

The roughness of its surface marked by shadows, the mountain behind Ca'Trestar did not, for no reason he could have quantified, threaten to collapse on to Alvarez; he did not suffer the mental fear of being crushed by it. All mountains could change character, but some did so only occasionally.

'A moment of quiet reflection, Inspector?'

He turned to face Varley, who had opened the door and was staring at him with amusement. He was sorry there appeared to be no way in which Varley could be linked with the murder.

'Presumably, you want to speak to Terry again?'

'Yes.'

'He's on the patio – a true devotee of Nidd. You will, of course, enjoy a drink, not suffering from the English belief that to imbibe before midday is to drink with the devil.'

The smooth bastard was insinuating he was a heavy drinker. He'd refuse, thus denying that slander and, if Varley had sufficient wit to understand, criticizing the quality of the brandy they offered their guests.

He followed Varley through the house and out on to the patio. Dale, stripped to the waist and wearing shorts, was seated in the full sun. When he recognized Alvarez, his expression soured.

'I have to leave you,' Varley said, 'but before I do, what can I offer you to drink?'

It occurred to Alvarez that if he did refuse the offer, it might seem to Varley that his earlier comments were responsible for the refusal. That would give the other false satisfaction. 'A *coñac*, please, with just ice.'

'Terry?'

'It's too early.'

One more snide comment?

Varley went indoors. Dale asked, with weak annoyance, 'What is it this time?'

'I have a few more questions to ask you, señor,' Alvarez answered.

'I've answered God knows how many already.'

'In a case like this, that is unfortunately inevitable.' Dale was not going to have the manners to suggest he sat, so he moved a patio chair into the shade.

'I don't know anything; I can't know anything.'

'Frequently, we find that a person does not realize how much he does know.'

Varley came out on to the patio, handed Alvarez a glass. 'I'm off, my duty done.'

'You won't . . .' Dale stopped.

'I'll be back before you even know I've gone.' He returned into the house.

Alvarez drank. One had to admit that on a hot day, even an inferior brandy was not to be despised too much. He noticed Dale was becoming increasingly nervous. Yet again, silence was a help.

'What exactly do you want?' Dale finally said, his voice high.

He let more time pass before he answered. 'You remember I told you Señor Mercer's car had been sabotaged?'

'Of course I do.'

'I have been finding out who could have been guilty and learned his car was usually left outside the garage at Villa Bellavista because there was difficulty in driving into and backing out of it. You understand what this means?'

'No.'

'It was very easy to sabotage a brake line when the car was there. That would not take long and since the road is not a busy one, the saboteur would have reason to think he had not been seen and identified, especially if he worked at night.'

'What's all this to do with me?'

'Did you go to Villa Bellavista and sabotage the car parked outside?'

'Of course I didn't.'

'You had cause to hate Señor Mercer.'

'Do I look like a murderer?'

'Few murderers look their part. One of the mildest-looking men I've met killed his wife and two children.'

'I never touched his car.'

'You told me you had never been to his house. That was a lie.'

'Yes, but . . . I've explained why I denied I had been there.'

'When a man lies once, it becomes easier to believe he is lying a second time.'

'I swear to God I never touched his car. I only went near his place that once.'

A false accusation sometimes provoked a genuine admission. 'I have been informed that when it was almost dark on the day before Señor Dale's death, you were seen by his car, apparently doing something to it.'

'That's ridiculous. I keep telling you, I've only been at his place that once.'

'It is a positive identification.'

'How can I make you understand it wasn't me?'

'I assured you there was no need for your wife to learn about your holiday here with Señor Varley, but sadly it is not always possible to honour one's assurances. Should it become necessary to make enquiries about you in England, it must be likely your wife will learn about your time here.'

He looked as if about to cry.

'Señor, I will ask you once more. Did you go one evening to Villa Bellavista and tamper with the car outside?'

'I swear I didn't.'

Alvarez finished the drink. As he stood, they heard a door slam and a moment later, Varley came out on to the patio. 'A social compliment to me, Inspector, or are you about to leave?'

'On this island, señor, to stand when someone enters is to imply the newcomer is not welcome.' He was gratified by Varley's brief expression of annoyance.

'He thinks I killed Steve,' Dale said wildly.

'How exciting!'

'Why do you talk so stupidly?'

'It's not exciting to be considered capable of murder?'

'You don't understand any more than he does.'

Alvarez understood it was unlikely Dale was the murderer. He said goodbye and left.

Twenty

Alvarez drove into Urbanización Bernejo and suffered the depression and sense of anger, he always experienced when concrete had replaced what had once been land covered with *garriga* in which had grown wild olive and evergreen oak trees. The north prided itself on being the most attractive part of the island; if building continued at its present rate, soon it would be difficult to justify such a description.

He parked outside Ca'n Federico, opened the rusting gate and walked past the solitary, sad hibiscus.

Osborn opened the door. 'Again?' he said dispiritedly. 'What do you want this time?'

'The answers to a few more questions. May I enter?'

Osborn stepped back and, silent, went into the sitting room. As Alvarez settled on one of the uncomfortable chairs, he wondered why Osborn had chosen to stay indoors where, lacking air-conditioning, it was hot and stuffy. 'Señor, I should like to know if you visited Señor Mercer's home on the day before he died?'

'I didn't.'

'You are certain?'

'Yes.'

'Do you remember what day he died on?'

There was no answer.

'Then how can you be certain you did not go there the previous day?'

'I didn't go there any day.'

'Not when you argued with him?'

'I meant after that.'

'You hated him, didn't you?'

'I didn't like him, that's all.'

'You hated him.'

'It's you saying that, not me.'

'You had every cause to hate him. You went to his house and asked him not to spoil your friendship with Señor Pollard. He laughed at you, called you objectionable names, enjoyed your mental pain. You would have to be superhuman not to hate him to the point of threatening him.'

'I did not threaten him.'

'Have you forgotten what you told me? That you became so angry you told him if he did not stop encouraging Señor Pollard, you would make him do so. Is that not a threat?'

'I said I didn't mean it like that.'

'He will have thought you did.'

'I was terribly upset.'

'Which is why you swore to get your own back.'

'I was just talking wildly.'

'You did not mean it?'

'Isn't that what I keep telling you?'

'I find that hard to believe.'

'Why?'

'Because I have been informed that on the evening before the crash, you were seen doing something to Señor Mercer's car, which was, as always, parked outside and not in the garage. Were you sabotaging the brakes?'

'For God's sake, I don't even know what car he had.'

'On the contrary, you made a point of identifying it so that you could be certain you were not damaging someone else's car.'

'You're twisting everything round.'

'No, señor, it is you who are the twister. Perhaps you

didn't mean to kill him. After all, how were you to guess he would be driving to Parelona along a road which can even kill the driver of a car whose brakes are in perfect order. Perhaps you hoped he would suffer just a small accident, hurt himself a little.'

'I couldn't have done anything.'

'Why not?'

'Because . . . When Tom stole the money and cleared off, I felt . . . You won't understand.'

'Until you explain.'

'I . . . I couldn't believe he'd left like that. I was scared he had had an accident and was in hospital. I went to his favourite bar and asked the staff if they'd seen him. One of them said he'd met someone, they'd had some drinks and had left together. I . . . I remembered Tom saying he needed more money than I had given him and how contemptuous and angry he became when I told him I couldn't afford it. I came back here and . . . just sat. I couldn't do anything.'

Alvarez remembered when Juana María had died, pinned against a wall by a drunken French driver. For many days afterwards he had been divorced from everybody and everything except the mental agony. He stood. 'The pain will take a long time to pass, señor, but eventually it will become just a sad memory.'

He left.

Alvarez reluctantly dialled Palma.

'Yes?' said Salas.

'I have to report that I have questioned Señor Osborn and Señor Dale.'

'Who?'

Alvarez hesitated, then said, 'Señor Osborn and Señor Dale are two possible suspects in the murder of Señor Mercer. I had no definite reason to believe either guilty, but in each case there were odd points concerning the evidence which needed checking out. In order to do this, I introduced false evidence, hoping to gain a definite impression when they were faced by this. In neither case did either—'

'Had you any positive indications?'

'I do not believe either was involved in the murder.'

'Whose murder?'

'Señor Mercer's.'

'Then kindly say so.'

'I did, earlier on.'

'What is the proof that neither was involved.'

'I can't say there is proof as such. You will know how difficult it is to prove a negative, that here there can be no evidence against either. I suppose a negative can only be proved, when something has not been said or done, when one is certain it would have been if all was as it should be. Even then, there is lack of evidence rather than presence of it, so that the negative is not exactly a positive, rather that the positive still might be negative . . .'

'Explore the outer bounds of verbal sanity no further. If you lack proof, on what are you basing your judgements?'

'The character of the two, their reactions to hostile questioning and, to a small extent, instinct.'

'You consider instinct to be a legitimate part of criminal investigation?'

'I think it can be, señor.'

'I suppose I should not be surprised.'

There was a silence.

'Well?'

'I think that's all, señor.'

'Since you have instinctively eliminated your only two suspects, where does your investigation now proceed?'

'I have been wondering if perhaps a negative means a

negative, señor.'

'And if a positive means a positive?'

'If none of the suspects is guilty, perhaps no one was.'

'And Señor Mercer is still alive despite being frozen in death?'

'I don't think you quite understand what I mean.'

'That surprises you?'

'Perhaps the crash was an accident.'

'That an expert has testified the brakes were sabotaged is of no account?'

'Experts can be wrong.'

'You mistakenly base that supposition on your own abilities?'

'Señor, have you heard from Credit Sempach regarding the money paid to Robert McCleary?'

'Until we can prove it was the result of criminal activity, they will tell us nothing. Since you cannot provide any positive evidence naming McCleary a criminal, cannot even be certain who he is, we have to accept the bank will make no disclosure.'

'If he wasn't Mercer, why would the letter have been in Mercer's possession?'

'You claim Mercer was McCleary on no evidence; that he was Faber, contrary to hard evidence that he was not; have you more pseudonyms to suggest, no doubt instinctively?'

Alvarez did not answer.

'If I were asked how this investigation could have been more incompetently carried out, I would not be able to answer,' Salas said, before he rang off.

Alvarez reached down to the bottom right-hand drawer of the desk.

Twenty-One

As he approached Sa Echona, Alvarez had still not decided whether to take Raquel to Restaurante Pinar or Restaurante Metropol. The chef at Pinar was the less gifted; the Metropol was more expensive. *Frito Mallorquin* at Pinar was tasty, *pato a la Sevillana* at Metropol was a dish to remember.

He parked, crossed to the ancient front door, knocked. Margarita welcomed him and showed him into the smaller sitting room, which had become tastefully elegant.

'You're ten minutes late,' Raquel said as he entered.

One counted only when one was very eager to meet an expected guest. How wrong Dolores had been about Raquel – a victim of her own sad memories. 'I'm sorry, but the car was trouble starting.'

'It had the temerity to thwart you for a while?'

It wasn't the first time she had, with tactful humour, recognized him as a man of authority.

'I know you would prefer a *coñac*, but I decided that, if we're going to celebrate, we should do it in style. Would you really mind having champagne?'

'Of course not.'

She turned to Margarita, who had remained in the doorway. 'Bring it with a couple of glasses, please.'

Was it Raquel's birthday, which meant he should have brought a present? But he was reasonably certain she had once casually mentioned she had been born in March.

Perhaps the cause of the celebration was simply that they were going out to dinner together.

'Before the end of the evening, Enrique, I want to talk to you about planting a small orchard of avocado pears. I suggested this to Rafael and he said the fruit would never ripen. Is that fact?'

'Far from it. Unless it's a very bad year, they do quite well on the island.'

'Then I will have my orchard, whatever Rafael says. Anything new positively scares him. It makes things so difficult and, to tell the truth, I keep thinking that if you . . . Well, there wouldn't be any complaining that because it wasn't done a hundred years ago, it can't be done now.'

He had little difficulty in divining what she had not said: if he were in command, the estate would flourish as never before. He'd work longer hours than any hired hand; he'd use all his inherited skill to make the land pour fourth its riches; when people spoke admiringly about Sa Echona, it would be because of his success.

Margarita returned with a bottle encased in a cooling jacket and two flutes. She put the salver down by the side of Raquel.

'No,' Raquel said, 'the man of the house.'

Margarita picked up the tray, crossed the room, set it down on the occasional table at Alvarez's side. She left.

'It had to be special, so I chose Krug.'

That meant nothing to him, but he expressed his delight. Sportsmen might open bottles of champagne and foolishly spray everyone within reach, but he was determined not to waste a drop of something she so clearly revered. He eased out the cork by turning the bottle around it, poured a little into each glass, waited until the bubbles had calmed, filled them, handed her one.

'Are you an expert in everything?' she asked.

'Ask my superior and he will tell you, in nothing.'

'Then he doesn't know you.' She raised her glass. 'To us.'

'To us,' he echoed. He drank. The champagne wasn't bad, but she had been correct: he would have preferred a good brandy.

'Where are we going to dine?'

'I was going to leave the choice to you.' As he was about to offer Pinar or Metropol, she forestalled him.

'As gallant as ever! I've heard so much about Sant Roc, I should love to go there.'

He suffered panic. Sant Roc had the reputation of being the best restaurant on the island, if not the whole of Spain. Such a reputation was earned by charging more for less. He had on him a hundred euros, which should have been more than enough, but now . . .

'It's almost at the other end of the island, which means it's quite a drive and it's supposed to be a little expensive, so perhaps you'd rather try somewhere else?'

Nothing would more humiliate him in her eyes than to admit he could not afford the restaurant of her choice. If he forewent a starter and a sweet, chose the cheapest main course (dieting? a doubtful stomach? a very heavy lunch?) and the *vino de casa* – assuming they had one – the bill surely could not be too shattering? Or could it? Should he say he had just remembered he had forgotten some work that would only take a moment to carry out, drive into the village and draw money from a cash machine? But the last time he had checked, there had been only a few euros left in his account. Would Dolores be able to lend him . . . Could anything be more absurd than to ask Dolores to lend him money to take Raquel to Sant Roc?

'You would prefer somewhere else? Perhaps a little smaller?'

'I was just working out the best route to take.'

* * *

The return journey was initially along the spine of the Sierra Tramuntana. The road twisted and turned and there were often unguarded drops beyond it; car brakes could lock, suspension collapse, engine seize, resulting in a fatal plunge down a precipitous slope. Only when they descended to the plain did he begin to relax. As if responding, she mumbled something and rested her head against his shoulder. The faint scent of expensive perfume caressed his nostrils. He might have an empty wallet, the waiter might have expressed silent contempt at the size of the tip, he might be hungry and thirsty, but the evening was proving to be as successful as he could have hoped.

He braked to a stop in front of Sa Echona. She pulled herself upright. 'Have I been asleep?'

'Perhaps just snoozing.'

'What poor company I've been.'

'The best company a man could have.'

She chuckled. 'You're becoming very gallant.' She raised her hand to look at her white-gold-and-diamond Piaget. 'Good grief, it's after one o'clock! I was going to ask you in for a last drink, but . . . Do you think it's too late?'

'Why should it be?'

'Entertaining a gentleman at this time of night can raise eyebrows.'

'Who's to know?'

'Margarita will certainly be fast asleep and snoring . . . Let's defy convention.'

He followed her into the house and through to the smaller sitting room.

'What are you going to drink? Your beloved *coñac*?'

'If I may.'

'I'll bring the bottle in.'

She left. He stared through the window and there was sufficient moonlight to make out some of the land beyond.

For much of his life he had longed to own land and farm it; he was within reach of realizing that dream.

She returned with a silver salver on which were a bottle, an empty glass, and a half-filled one. She put it down on an occasional table. 'Help yourself. And don't be shy.'

Shy about how much he poured? Or shy about speaking out? He crossed to the table, handed her the half-filled glass, poured himself a notably generous brandy – he was feeling nervous.

'To us,' she said, as he sat.

'To us.' He drank deeply.

'It's been great fun. We must do it again and perhaps next time you will be feeling much better and can have a proper meal.'

Depending on who paid.

'You've explained how the estate could be restored. That's something you could do, isn't it?'

'I . . . I think so.'

'I know so.'

She had declared herself, yet he was still too nervous to come directly to the point. 'There need to be many more algarroba trees, because the beans are becoming a valuable crop. Seeds need to be bought abroad, perhaps from England, to ensure fresh strains. One must take account of the changes in culture that foreigners have introduced. Sweet corn used to be for pigs; now the locals are learning to enjoy it. With so much land, many sheep can be grazed. The English breed Suffolk should be introduced because they produce very good carcasses. I don't think the land is suitable for wine grapes, but the Institute of Agriculture can be consulted.'

'It's all exciting. So when can you start? I hate talking money, so you'll have to speak to the lawyers about your salary.'

'Salary?'

She smiled. 'Surely you are not so enthusiastic as to want to work for nothing?' She studied him. 'You didn't think . . . Oh, dear, I believe you did. Surely you realize how impossible that would be?'

'Why?' he asked hoarsely.

'In my position in life, I could hardly marry someone in yours.'

He sat at the table and drank. There were footsteps on the stairs and Dolores, wearing a dressing gown, appeared.

She stepped down on to the floor, arms folded, and studied him. 'I heard sounds and awoke Jaime and told him to find out if we were being burgled. He was so certain it was only mice, I had to come down myself. And what do I find? You, drinking at an hour when every respectable person is asleep in bed.'

'I'm sorry I woke you.'

'You should be.'

'I needed a drink.'

'Obviously.'

'I'm sorry I woke you.'

'Alcohol has blanketed your memory. You have already apologized. Do you intend to remain here and drink until you no longer have a memory?'

'Would that that could happen.'

'You are not drinking because you have already drunk too much?'

He shook his head. He fiddled with the glass. 'You were right,' he said in a low voice.

For once she forbade to remark that she always was. 'I was right about Raquel?'

'Yes.'

She uncrossed her arms, modestly made certain the dressing gown was fully closed, then sat. 'Poor Enrique.'

There was a call from upstairs. 'What's going on?'

They ignored the question.

Jaime came down the stairs. Lacking his wife's sense of decorum, he wore only a pair of pyjama trousers. 'Having a drink, are we?'

'You are not,' she snapped.

'But—'

'You are going back to bed.'

He hesitated, then returned upstairs.

'Now,' she said as she faced Alvarez, 'tell me all that happened.'

Twenty-Two

'Have you made the slightest progress?' Salas asked.

Yes, Alvarez thought bitterly. He had succeeded in making a humiliated fool of himself.

'Are you still there?'

'Yes, señor.'

'Then why don't you answer?'

'I was arranging my mind.'

'An impossible task. Now kindly tell me: have you made any progress?'

'No, señor.'

'Why not?'

Because all that now concerned him was how he could have been so blinded? Had greed, the greed for land, played its part? 'The facts are complex.'

'Not least because of your absurd insistence that the dead man is alive with a dozen identities.'

'I am certain Mercer . . .'

'Was not Faber.'

'Unless . . .'

'Unless one can believe that those working in the English police force are even half as incompetent as you.'

'The payment acknowledgement from Credit Sempach in an envelope addressed to McCleary proves—'

'Proves nothing except to one who is sufficiently incompetent to conduct a case solely on assumptions.'

'The book was in Mercer's room.'

'Can you prove it was not lent to him or was one he had bought second hand and the letter was used as a bookmarker and was forgotten?'

'Would one forget such a letter? Isn't that rather an unlikely assumption?'

'You do yourself no service with your insolent question.'

'Señor, have you spoken to England about their identification of the photo?'

'Of course I have not.'

'And the passport?'

'Was genuine and issued in good faith. It is quite clear you have failed to use any intelligence in this case. You will question everyone again, study every aspect of the case again, and you will not rest until you have made progress. Is that clear?'

'Yes, señor.'

Salas did not bother to say goodbye. Alvarez slumped back in his chair. Would Raquel amuse all her rich friends with stories about the clown of a detective who had been sufficiently presumptuous to believe she would marry him? Had she humiliated him because that would hurt Dolores or because she despised him? What did it matter? Life was not designed to be sweet. But did it have to be so bitter?

The bartender in Club Llueso said, 'You look like your execution is in an hour's time. Is your boss trying to discover if you've done any work in the past ten years?'

'I want a coffee and a *coñac*.'

'You're good at telling what you want, not so good at asking politely.'

Twenty minutes and three brandies later Alvarez returned to his car, settled behind the wheel, switched on the fan to try to clear some of the heat and stared through the windscreen at a passing donkey cart, a sight once very familiar, now rare. Salas was demanding he solve the case, working no matter how many hours a day. It was so easy to give orders and assume the truth was out there waiting to be discovered. But sometimes the truth had vanished. There could come the point in a case where the logical man accepted he would never solve it and turned to other problems; but it was hopeless to ask Salas to be logical. So he must question everyone yet again, search Mercer's rooms again, try to uncover enough evidence to persuade Credit Sempach to give details of the account in McCleary's name and when all that failed he could honestly say to Salas that he had done everything that was possible but to no effect.

He drove out of the village and on to the Palma road, turned off that on to the Playa Neuva road and continued to Villa Bellavista. The house was locked and shuttered, proving that when one thing went wrong, so did everything else. He returned to his car, started the engine, backed. The blast of a horn caused him to start and slam on the brakes. When he looked in the rear-view mirror, he saw Susan climbing out of her car.

She came across. 'Don't you ever look where you're going?'

'I'm sorry. It was entirely my fault.'

'Admitting you were in the wrong to a woman driver? You do run true to form, don't you?'

'How do you mean?'

'What do you want here?'

'To have a word with you. I'm sorry, but I have to ask more questions.'

'But never the right ones.'

He wondered why she was speaking so antagonistically.

'Then let's get it over with. I have to prepare this place for the new load of tourists.'

By the time he was out of the car, she was unlocking the front door. He crossed, stepped inside. 'I presume your husband is not here?'

'Disappointed?'

'I'll have to have a word with him as well.'

'You'll be wasting your time.'

'Why's that?'

'Because he's already found himself another boyfriend.'

Her words made no sense unless . . . unless she thought he was . . . 'You think I'm interested?'

'I'm not blind.'

'That's ridiculous.'

'Is it? When you've carefully kept a mile away from me every time I've given hints.'

'You're married.'

'You think I'd marry Dick?' she asked contemptuously. 'I'd as soon shack up with you and sleep on my own.'

His mind went into orbit. Raquel had treated him with contempt; now Susan was doing the same. He could not lessen Raquel's contempt, but he could erase the cause for Susan's. He grasped her, kissed her, let his hands wander.

'Upstairs will be a lot more comfortable,' she murmured.

They went into the first bedroom. She unzipped her dress and pulled it up and over her head, dropped it on a chair. She reached behind herself, unclipped her brassière, put it down on her dress. 'You're a cunning bastard.'

'Why say that?' he asked thickly.

'You didn't stay clear because you thought I was married. You wanted to make me desperate.'

He might have commented, had he not been intent on watching her step out of her pants.

They sat on the uncomfortable chairs in the sitting room. He finished his brandy, put the glass down.

'Another?' she asked.

'As soon as you like.'

She laughed. 'The complete fraud! But one hell of a man. Right now, what I'm offering you is another drink.'

'I'll get it.'

'You need to conserve your energy.' She stood, crossed and kissed him, picked up his glass and went through to the kitchen.

Later – some time later – he persuaded her it would be more advantageous to both of them if she answered a few questions before anything more; then their pleasure would be unalloyed. 'Why did you say to me, "You think I'd marry Dick?"'

'Surely that's obvious?'

'I'll put it another way. Why pretend you were married to him?'

'What's it matter?'

'I don't know until you give me the answer.'

'Forget it.'

'When I know the answer.'

'Do you have to go on and on?'

'I have to try to identify who killed Mercer.'

After a while, she said, 'I'm scared. I'm scared of you.'

'Why?'

'Because you're like a dog that's got its teeth into someone and won't let go . . . I didn't have anything to do with it.'

'With what?'

'Steve's death. You must believe me.'

'Why should I disbelieve you?'

'At first, I just thought it was some kind of a stupid joke until . . . Even then, I didn't think it could . . . I wouldn't have agreed, however much he offered.'

'Agreed to what?'

'To come out here and make out I was married to him.'

'I think we'll have another drink and then you had better tell me exactly what has been happening.'

After leaving home, she had led a careless life, enjoying its good times and with little thought there might be bad times ahead. Fashion had taken a sharp turn and her style of beauty was suddenly not much in demand. Owe a million pounds and it's the lender who sweats; owe a thousand pounds and it's you. Creditors had harried her until she became scared she would end up on the streets. Then she had met Thorne. He'd offered her enough money to pay off her debts, and more, provided she would live with him as his wife in Mallorca. Betty, her best friend, had warned her that she'd be a fool to agree. Betty did not owe money everywhere and especially to one person who did not mind how he gained repayment. She had very soon learned that her instinctive judgement of Thorne had been correct. She would not be called upon to make repayment with her body. Her cost was increasing frustration, boredom, and unfulfilled desire – Thorne had warned her there were to be no affairs. There was also the resentment of having to work for tourists who were sometimes pleasant, more usually indifferent, occasionally bloody rude.

'Why did he want you to work for the letting agency?'

For a while she had been curious about that and had even asked him, but his anger at the question had taught her to accept things as they were. He had wanted her to do the work, she did it. Just as Steve had done what he had been told . . .

'Was Mercer Steve's real name?'

'He said it was, and that's what was on his passport, but once I saw him with a letter addressed to someone else.'

'Can you remember what the name was?'

'Something like MacCloud.'

'McCleary?'

'Yes. How did you know that?'

'When did you come out here?'

'September.'

'Of last year?'

'Has to be, doesn't it, since it's only May now.'

'But . . .'

'You don't believe me?'

'I believe you. I'm just trying to make sense of all you're telling me.' And then he remembered the many trips Faber had made to his elderly aunt.

'You and Thorne came out here together?'

'Yes.'

'And Mercer?'

'The same.'

'But at first Thorne wasn't here all the time?'

'Came out for weekends.'

'Then who did the gardening?'

'During the week? Someone he'd got hold of – a Romanian. The letting agency didn't mind so long as the work was done. Most times they didn't know who was doing it.'

'When you met Thorne in England, did he have a gammy leg?'

'No.'

'And his hair was light brown; he didn't appear to be going bald?'

'That's how he was.'

'And when he came out here, he was wearing a wig of black hair?'

'Yeah, but he doesn't wear a wig now. His hair is black.'

'Dyed. Did the changes make you wonder what the reason was?'

She shrugged her shoulders. 'If you mean the hair, these days anything can happen. They shave it all off, dye it, plait it. Just thought he was trying to make himself out to be younger and better-looking than he was.'

'It didn't occur to you he might be engaged in a criminal activity?'

'Of course it didn't. I wouldn't have stayed if it had.'

Perhaps. 'Did you notice a strange likeness between Steve and Dick?'

'There was a kind of similarity between them, but you'd never mistake the one for the other, would you? I mean, him with that gammy leg. Have you got to go on and on asking questions?'

'I think I've reached the end of them.'

'Then let's do something more interesting.' She stood, then crossed the room to the doorway.

As he followed her, he thought that if Raquel had not humiliated him, he would not have broken the barrier of 'marriage' in his mind. If that had not happened, Susan would not have told him all she had. It was not only God who moved in mysterious ways; life did the same

'Are you going to sit there, staring into space?'

He hurriedly followed her upstairs.

Twenty-Three

Alvarez walked into the kitchen at nine o'clock on Sunday. Jaime dunked a piece of *coca* into a mugful of hot chocolate. 'We thought you must have fallen over and broken your neck.'

'I thought no such thing,' Dolores corrected sharply. 'Had I done so, I would have phoned the police and the hospitals.' She spoke to Alvarez. 'I suppose you want some breakfast?'

'If it is no trouble.'

'Only a man could speak so stupidly. Of course it is trouble. But that is all a woman ever knows.'

'You missed a good supper last night,' Jaime said.

'Of small matter when he had a far better one elsewhere,' Dolores observed.

'All I had was cold meat and salad,' Alvarez said.

'Margarita was away?'

'I was not at Raquel's. In any case, what if Margarita wasn't there?'

'I can understand that you, being a man, have never asked yourself if it is Raquel who does the cooking about which she boasts. Why should you care if Margarita slaves while Raquel claims the credit? Like all men, you are content to eat and are indifferent as to who spent hours preparing the food.'

'Why do you say Raquel doesn't do the cooking?'

'Because she is too lazy even to boil an egg. What I

cannot understand is how you could have returned there after what happened. Any woman, even the meanest, would have had far too much pride to do so. Sadly, a man has no pride.'

'I did not eat at Sa Echona.'

'That you could accept her hospitality, having discovered the bitch she is . . . I cannot believe it.'

'That's the first sensible thing you've said. Yesterday evening, I was questioning a witness.'

'You ask me to believe you would miss my meal from a sense of duty?'

'She invited me to stay on, so I did, hoping that would make her more willing.'

'You shame me with such talk.'

'Willing to answer questions.'

'Since you did not return during the night, there can be no doubt what her answers were. As my mother would say, the many times she needed to console herself, "A woman must look to heaven for her reward."'

'What if she goes down to hell?' Jaime asked.

'She finds herself among men too lazy to do anything but talk and drink,' she snapped.

Alvarez stared through the unshuttered window of the office at the harsh sunlight on the wall of the building opposite. Being the first day of the working week meant Monday was always dark. This Monday was black. He had to report to Salas and try to explain the facts.

He had been right repeatedly to face Salas's scorn and claim Mercer was Faber – not in practical terms, it was true, but as a fall guy. Faber, unlike so many criminals, had accepted that however much care he took in planning, Sod's Law might interrupt. So how to counter that danger as far as possible? The moment the theft was recognized, the police would be searching for him, so he planned a double deception.

He created an aunt who lived in Birmingham, whom he visited regularly because he was so concerned about her well-being. That explained to any nosy neighbour why he was so often away from home. The police would try to identify her and it would take time and effort to do this; when they failed, resources would be diverted to cases which offered a chance of contributing to a better clear-up rate.

He had needed to find two accomplices, a man and a woman, who needed money and would not be over-concerned how they made it. He had soon met Susan, but it must have taken longer to find Mercer/McCleary because he had to bear a recognizable similarity to himself. The thinking behind this was complex. Accepting Sod's Law meant that despite all the precautions he took, including the absence of any photograph of himself, the police might learn he had fled to Mallorca. (They had. Not because of Sod's Law, but from his forgetting the postman). If that happened, a description of him would be broadcast and a search made. Since Mercer did to some degree resemble him, some fool (Inspector Alvarez) might convince himself he had made a definite identification. England would be consulted. They would negate the identification. Inevitably, this failure would result in Mercer's being rejected as a possible suspect. (A mistake. That fool inspector might not have the intelligence to act logically. Sod's Law.)

Each visit to the island had been made on a passport in the name of Thorne – he had never applied for one in his own name so there was no file photograph. As Thorne, he had travelled in disguise. Not a disguise, as sometimes portrayed, so brilliant it would never be penetrated even by those who studied bone structure, relative positions of physical features, etc., but one that was practical and could later be incorporated into a permanent appearance. A wig of black hair – a small fortune would buy a wig not easily identified as such – a limp resulting from a car accident, mannerisms which bore no relation to any of Faber's which might have been recorded, and, most important of all, a menial job. Who was going to look for a man who had stolen a fortune doing jobbing gardening? A rich man led a rich life.

When enquiries had begun, Mercer and Susan had been told to direct the investigating detective's interest on to others. Had there been further evidence to implicate either Osborn or Dale, that might have carried far more weight than it eventually did. It was human nature that was going to defeat Faber/Thorne. McCleary, to give Mercer that name, had been paid with money deposited in Credit Sempach. Had he been content with the agreed amount, the search for Faber would have died; no force was going to work for very long on a case dumped on it from abroad which was becoming more and more unlikely to be solved. But he was greedy and, far more street-wise than Susan, had judged the deception covered not stupidity but a criminal activity in which Faber had made a great deal of money; perhaps he had read about the theft and put two and two together. So Thorne would pay him more, much more, than had been agreed, or the police would learn what was going on. Thorne had refused to pay, so Mercer had had to die and, ironically as far as he was concerned, this had brought the case sharply alive. And because it had, Alvarez had questioned Susan yet again and as a consequence of that . . .

He reached down to the bottom right-hand drawer of the desk, brought out the bottle of brandy and a glass. He needed inspiration. How to explain events which had led him to the truth to someone as prudish as Salas? The superior chief was probably under the misapprehension that pillow talk was an elderly husband asking his wife to make some tea.